Unearthly Fire

Sirius crouched, his eyes blazing, baying defiance and anger.

"What's going on?" The cat Tibbles was on the back of the sofa in a white and spitting arch.

"Get down!" Sirius bayed at her.

New-Sirius swung an impatient blow toward the sofa. Blue-green flame smickered. And Tibbles vanished.

"What's happening? Oh, *where's* the light?"

Now it was Kathleen. Sirius could see her, dim and white, fumbling at the wall by the door for the light switch. After what had happened to Tibbles, Sirius knew she wasn't safe. He wasn't going to let anyone kill Kathleen. The idea filled him with green rage. He burst out from under the side of the table and sprang for the attacker's throat....

Other Bullseye Books you will enjoy

Charmed Life by Diana Wynne Jones
A Tale of Time City by Diana Wynne Jones
Witch Week by Diana Wynne Jones
The Phantom Tollbooth by Norton Juster
Chitty-Chitty-Bang-Bang by Ian Fleming

Dogsbody

Dogsbody

DIANA WYNNE JONES

BULLSEYE BOOKS • ALFRED A. KNOPF
New York

DR. M. JERRY WEISS, Distinguished Service Professor of Communications at Jersey City State College, is the educational consultant for Bullseye Books. A past chair of the International Reading Association President's Advisory Committee on Intellectual Freedom, he travels frequently to give workshops on the use of trade books in schools.

Library of Congress Catalog Card Number: 76-28714
ISBN: 0-394-82031-2
RL: 5.7
First Bullseye edition: February 1990

Manufactured in the United States of America
1 2 3 4 5 6 7 8 9 10

For Caspian,
who might really be Sirius

Dogsbody

1 THE DOG STAR stood beneath the Judgment Seats and raged. The green light of his fury fired the assembled faces viridian. It lit the underside of the rooftrees and turned their moist blue fruit to emerald.

"None of this is *true!*" he shouted. "Why can't you believe *me,* instead of listening to *him?*" He blazed on the chief witness, a blue luminary from the Castor complex, firing him turquoise. The witness backed hastily out of range.

"Sirius," the First Judge rumbled quietly, "we've already found you guilty. Unless you've anything reasonable to say, be quiet and let the Court pass sentence."

"No I will *not* be quiet!" Sirius shouted up at the huge ruddy figure. He was not afraid of Antares. He had often sat beside him as Judge on those same Judgment Seats— that was one of the many miserable things about this trial. "You haven't listened to a word I've said, all through. I did *not* kill that luminary—I only hit him. I was *not* negligent, and I've offered to look for the Zoi. The most you can accuse me of is losing my temper—"

"Once too often, in the opinion of this Court," remarked big crimson Betelgeuse, the Second Judge, in his dry way.

"And I've admitted I lost my temper," said Sirius.

"No one would have believed you if you hadn't," said Betelgeuse.

A long flicker of amusement ran around the assembled luminaries. Sirius glared at them. The hall of blue trees was packed with people from every sphere and all orders of effulgence. It was not often one of the high effulgents was on trial for his life—and there never had been one so notorious for losing his temper.

"That's right—laugh!" Sirius roared. "You're getting what you came for, aren't you? But you're not watching justice done. I tell you I'm not guilty! I don't know who killed that young fool, but it wasn't *me!*"

"The Court is not proposing to go through all that again," Antares said. "We have your Companion's evidence that you often get too angry to know what you're doing."

Sirius saw his Companion look at him warningly. He pretended not to see her. He knew she was trying to warn him not to prove the case against him by raging any more. She had admitted only a little more than anyone knew. She had not really let him down. But he was afraid he would never see her again, and he knew it would make him angrier than ever to look at her. She was so beautiful: small, exquisite and pearly.

"If I were up there, I wouldn't call that evidence," he said.

"No, but it bears out the chief witness," said Antares, "when he says he surprised you with the body and you tried to kill him by throwing the Zoi at him."

"I didn't," said Sirius. He could say nothing more. He

could only stand fulminating because his case was so weak. He refused to tell the Court that he had threatened to kill the blue Castor-fellow for hanging around his Companion, or that he had struck out at the young luminary for gossiping about it. None of that proved his innocence anyway.

"Other witnesses saw the Zoi fall," said Antares. "Not to speak of the nova sphere—"

"Oh go to blazes!" said Sirius. "Nobody else saw anything."

"Say that again," Betelgeuse put in, "and we'll add contempt of court to the other charges. Your entire evidence amounts to contempt anyway."

"Have you anything more to say?" asked Antares. "Anything, that is, which isn't a repetition of the nonsense you've given us up to now?"

Rather disconcerted, Sirius looked up at the three Judges, the two red giants and the smaller white Polaris. He could see they all thought he had not told the full story. Perhaps they were hoping for it now. "No, I've nothing else to say," he said. "Except that it was *not* nonsense. I—"

"Then be quiet while our spokesman passes the sentence," said Antares.

Polaris rose, quiet, tall and steadfast. Being a Cepheid, he had a slight stammer, which would have disqualified him as spokesman, had not the other two Judges been of greater effulgence. "D-denizen of S-sirius," he began.

Sirius looked up and tried to compose himself. He had not had much hope all through, and none since they declared him guilty. He had thought he was quite prepared. But now the sentence was actually about to come, he felt sick. This trial had been about whether he, Sirius, lived or died. And it seemed only just to have occurred to him that it was.

"This Court," said Polaris, "has f-found you guilty on three counts, namely: of m-murdering a young luminary s-stationed in Orion; of grossly m-misusing a Zoi to com-m-mit that s-said m-murder; and of culpable negligence, causing t-trepidation, irregularity and d-damage in your entire s-sphere of inf-fluence and l-leading t-to the l-loss of the Z-zoi." For the moment, his stammer fazed him, and he had to stop.

Sirius waited. He tried to imagine someone else as denizen of his green sphere, and could not. He looked down, and tried not to think of anything. But that was a mistake. Down there, through the spinning star-motes of the floor, he looked into nothing. He was horrified. It was all he could do not to scream at them not to make him into nothing.

Polaris recovered himself. "In p-passing this s-sentence," he said, "the Court takes into cons-sideration your high eff-ffulgency and the s-services you have f-formerly rendered the Court. In view of these, and the f-fact that you are l-liable to rages in which you cannot be s-said to be in your right m-mind, the Court has d-decided to revive an ancient p-prerogative to p-pass a s-special kind of s-suspended s-sentence."

What was this? Sirius did not know what to think. He looked at his Companion, and then wished he had not, because of the doubt and consternation he saw in her.

"D-denizen of S-sirius," said Polaris, "you are hereby s-sentenced to be s-stripped of all s-spheres, honors and eff-ffulgences and banished f-from here to the body of a creature native to that s-sphere where the m-missing Z-zoi, is thought to have f-fallen. If, d-during the life s-span of that creature, you are able to f-find and retrieve the Z-zoi, the Court will be p-pleased to reinstate you in all your f-former s-spheres and d-dignities. F-failure to retrieve the Z-zoi will carry no f-further p-punishment. In the Court's op-opinion, it is s-sufficient that you s-simply die in the m-manner natural to creatures of that s-sphere."

Slow as Polaris was in giving this extraordinary sentence, Sirius had still barely grasped it when Polaris sat down. It was unheard of. It was worse than nothing, because it condemned him not only to exile but hope—hopeless, brutish hope, over a whole uncertain life span. He flared up again as he realized it.

"But that's the most preposterous sentence I ever heard!"

"Quiet," said Antares. "The Court orders the prisoner taken away and the sentence carried out."

"Try saying *preposterous*, Polaris!" Sirius shouted as they led him away.

The sentence was carried out at once. When he came to himself, Sirius was no longer capable of protesting. He could not see clearly, or speak. Nor did he think much, either. He was very weak and very, very hungry. All his strength had to be spent fighting for food among a warm bundle of creatures like himself. He had just found himself a satisfactory slot and was feeding, when he felt himself plucked off again by a large invincible hand and turned upside down. He made noises in protest, and kicked a little.

A great gruff voice, probably a woman's, said words he did not understand. "That's the sixth beastly dog in this litter. To one bitch. Blast it!"

Sirius was plunked unceremoniously back, and fought his way to his slot again. He did not think much about anything but feeding for quite a while after that. Then he slept, wedged warmly among the other creatures, against a great hairy cliff. It was some days before he thought about anything but food and sleep.

But at length he was seized with an urge to explore. He set off, crawling strenuously on four short legs which seemed far too weak to carry his body. He tripped several times over the folds in the rough cloth he was crawling on. The other creatures were crawling vaguely about, too. More than once, Sirius was bowled over by one. But he kept on, blinking, trying to see where the strong light was coming from a little farther off. He came to cold floor, where crawling was easier.

He was nearly in the strong, warm light, when footsteps clacked toward him. The ground shook. He stopped uncertainly. Once again, he was seized by something ineffably strong and turned upward, kicking and undignified, toward a vaguely looming face. "You're a bold one," remarked the great gruff woman's voice. Then, as Sirius blinked, trying

to see what had caught him, the voice said, "I don't like
the look of your eyes, fellow. Something tells me Bess has
been a naughty girl."

Since he understood none of the sounds the gruff voice
made, Sirius felt nothing but exasperation when he was
put back in the dark on the rough cloth. Now he would
have all that crawling to do again. He waited for the heavy
footsteps to clack away, and then set off again.

It did no good. He was put back by someone—either the
woman or a being with a hoarse youth's voice—every time
he reached the light. He cheeped with frustration. Something in him craved for that light. Why would they not
let him have it?

He was in the doorway the next day, when they came—
the woman, the hoarse youth and another person. They
nearly trod on him. Sirius knew it, and cowered down in
terror. The woman, with an exclamation of annoyance,
plucked him up from the cold floor into the light.

"Blast this one! It *is* a wanderer." Sirius was quite used to
being picked up by this time. He lay quiet. "Well?" said
the woman. "What do you think, Mrs. Canning dear?
Those markings aren't right, are they? And look at its
eyes."

Sirius felt the attention of the other person on him. It
felt wrong, somehow. He struggled, and was firmly squeezed
for his pains. "No," said a new voice thoughtfully, and it
troubled Sirius. It and the smell that went with it set up a
ripple that was nearly a memory in his head. "Wrong eyes,
wrong color ears. Your bitch must have got out somehow,

Mrs. Partridge dear. What are the others like?"

"The same, with variations. Take a look."

There were indignant cheepings that told Sirius that his companions, less used to being handled than he, were being bundled about too. Above the noise, the three voices held a long discussion. And below the cheeping, there was a deeper, anxious whining.

"Shut up, Bess! You've been a bad girl!" said the voice called Mrs. Partridge. "So you don't think these'll fetch any money at all?"

"You might get a pound or so from a pet shop," said the voice called Mrs. Canning. "Otherwise—"

"Much obliged!" Mrs. Partridge said. There was such an unmistakable note of anger in her voice that Sirius cringed and his companions stopped cheeping. They were silent when they were plunked back on the ground, though one or two whimpered plaintively when the big anxious mother licked them. The footsteps went away, but two sets of them returned, briskly and angrily, not long after. All the puppies cringed instinctively.

"Blast you, Bess!" said Mrs. Partridge. "Here I am with a parcel of mongrels, when I might have got nearly a hundred quid for this litter. Got that sack, Brian?"

"Uh-huh." The hoarse youth never used many words. "Brick too. Oughtn't we to leave her one, Mrs. Partridge?"

"Oh, I suppose so," the woman said impatiently. Sirius felt himself seized and lifted. "Not that one!" Mrs. Partridge said sharply. "I don't like its eyes."

"Don't you?" The youth seemed surprised, but he dumped

Sirius down again and picked up the next nearest to set beside the mother. The mother whined anxiously, but she did not try to stop him as he seized the other puppies one by one and tossed them into dusty, chaffy darkness. They tumbled in anyhow, cheeping and feebly struggling. Sirius was carried, one of this writhing, squeaking bundle, pressed and clawed by his fellows, jolted by the movement of the sack, until he was nearly frantic. Then a new smell broke through the dust. Even in this distress it interested him. But, the next moment, their bundle swung horribly and dropped, more horribly still, into cold, cold, cold. To his terror, there was nothing to breathe but the cold stuff, and it choked him.

Once he realized it choked him, Sirius had the sense to stop breathing. But there was not much sense to the way he struggled. For as long as he had air and strength in his body, he lashed out with all his short weak legs, tore with his small feeble claws, and fought the darkness and the cold as if it were a live enemy. Some of the other puppies fought too, and got in one another's way. But, one by one, they found the shock and the cold suffocation too much for them. Soon only Sirius was scratching and tearing at the dark, and he only kept on because he had a dim notion that anything was better than cold nothingness.

The darkness opened. Sirius did not care much about anything by then, but he thought he was probably dead. Being dead seemed to mean floating out into a gray-green light. It was not a light he could see by, and it was stronger above him. He had a feeling he was soaring toward the stronger light. Round bubbles, shining yellow, moved up past his eyes and put him in mind of another life he could not quite remember. Then the light was like a silver lid, thick and solid-looking overhead. It surprised him when he broke through the silver without pain or noise into a huge brightness that was blue and green and warm. It was too much for him. He took a gasping breath, choked and became nothing more than a sodden wisp of life floating down a brisk river.

Behind him, at the bottom of the river, the rotten sack he had torn spread apart in the current and the other sodden wisps floated out. Two were beyond hope and were simply rolled along the mud and stones of the riverbed. But four other wisps rose to the surface and were carried along behind the first. They went bobbing and twisting, one behind the other, around a bend in the river and between the sunny banks of a meadow. Here, the warmth beating from above began to revive Sirius a little. He came to himself enough to know that there was heat somewhere, and that he was helpless in some kind of nightmare. The only good thing in the nightmare was the heat. He came to depend on it.

The river passed hawthorn trees growing on its banks. The current carried Sirius through the shadow of one. He found himself suddenly in deep brown cold. The heat was gone. They had taken his one comfort away now. He was so indignant about it that he opened his eyes and tried to cheep a protest.

He could not manage a noise. But a second later, the

river carried him out into sunlight again. Sun struck him full in the eyes and broke into a thousand dazzles on the ripples. Sirius snapped his eyes shut again. The brightness was such a shock that he became a limper wisp than ever and hardly knew that the warmth was back again.

It grew warmer—a golden, searching warmth. "It *is* you, Effulgency!" someone said. "I thought it was!"

This was quite a different order of voice from those Sirius had heard so far. It puzzled him. It was not a voice he knew, though he had a feeling he had heard its kind before. He was not sure he trusted it. All the voices he had heard so far had done him nothing but harm—and he had a notion he had known voices before that, which had done him no good either.

"You aren't dead, are you?" the voice asked. It seemed anxious. It was a warm, golden voice, and, though it sounded anxious, there was a hint of ferocity about it, as if the speaker could be far more dangerous than Mrs. Partridge and her friends if he chose.

Sirius was not sure if he was dead or not. He felt too weak to cope with this strong, fierce voice, so he floated on in silence.

"Can't you answer?" The warmth playing on Sirius's scrap of body grew stronger and hotter, as if the speaker was losing patience. Sirius was too far gone even to be frightened. He simply floated. "I suppose you can't," said the voice. "I think this is just too bad of them! Well, I'll do what I can for you. Just let them try to stop me!"

The warmth stayed, lapping around Sirius, though he

sensed that the speaker had gone. He floated a little way farther, until he came up against some things that were long, green and yielding. Here the warmth caught and pinned him, gently rocking. It was almost pleasant. Meanwhile, the other four half-drowned puppies floated on in midstream, around bends, to where the river became wider and dirtier, with houses on its banks.

A shrill voice spoke strange words near Sirius, "Oh, eughky! There's a dead puppy in the rushes!"

"Don't touch it!" said a voice rather older and rougher. And a third voice, gentle and lilting, said, "Let me see!"

"Don't touch it, Kathleen!" said the second voice.

However, there were splashings and rustlings. A pair of hands, a great deal smaller and much more shaky and nervous than Sirius was used to, picked him out of the water and held him high in the air. He did not feel safe. The shakiness of those hands and the cold air frightened him. He wriggled and managed to utter a faint squeak of fear. The hands all but dropped him.

"It isn't dead! It's *alive!* Poor thing, it's *frozen!*"

"Someone tried to drown it," said the shrillest voice.

"Throw it back in," said the second voice. "It's too small to lap. It'll die anyway."

"No it won't." The hands holding Sirius became defiantly steady. "It can have that old baby bottle. I'm not going to let it die."

"Mum won't let you keep it," the rough voice said nastily.

"She won't. And the cats'll kill it," said the youngest voice. "Honest, Kathleen."

The girl holding Sirius hugged him defensively to her chest and began to walk—bump, jerk, bump—away from the river across the meadow. "Poor little thing," she said. The two boys followed, arguing with her. Their clamor hurt Sirius's ears, and the girl kept jerking him by turning around to argue back. But he realized she was defending him from the other two and was grateful. Her convulsive hugging was making him feel safer and a great deal warmer. "Oh!" Kathleen exclaimed, bending over him. "Its tail's wagging!"

Robin, the younger boy, demanded to see. "It's a queer little tail," he said doubtfully. "You don't think it's really a rat, do you?"

"No," said Kathleen. "It's a dog."

"It's a rat," said Basil, the elder boy. "An Irish rat. Shamus O'Rat!"

"Shut up," Kathleen said wearily.

2

SIRIUS WAS brought somewhere warm, and tenderly put in a basket. He went to sleep. As he slept, his draggled coat dried and became slightly curly. The hair on his reddish lapped-over ears dried last of all, and then he was truly comfortable. He woke up, stretching his back pair of legs and his front hard and straight, to find there were hostile, alien things nearby.

These creatures did not speak. They had no language exactly. But they felt things so firmly and acutely that Sirius knew what they meant just as if they had spoken.

"What is it? It doesn't smell nice."

Sirius's nose twitched. He did not care for the way these creatures smelled either, come to that.

"It's one of those things that bark and chase you up trees."

"Are you sure? It doesn't look big enough."

"That"—with great contempt—"is because it's a baby still. It'll grow."

"They'd no business to bring it to our house!"

"It had better not chase *us* up trees!"

"Let's get rid of it before it can."

"We certainly will, the first chance we get. Don't have anything to do with it till then. It's beneath our notice."

"Shoo! Get out, Tibbles. Buzz off, Romulus and Remus." Kathleen and Robin came to kneel down beside the basket. The queer creatures vanished, in unmistakable disdain and annoyance. Sirius wagged his tail. Then he opened his eyes and tried to see what his two rescuers looked like. They were so big that he found it hard to focus on them.

"Funny tail!" said Kathleen, laughing.

"Funny *eyes!*" said Robin. "Kathleen, its eyes are green. Dogs don't have green eyes, do they? Do you think it's something else?"

"I know it's a puppy," said Kathleen.

"Basil's going to say it's a cat," said Robin. "He'll call it Shamus O'Cat, I know he will."

"Let him," Kathleen said recklessly. It was the only way she could express the feeling the puppy's eyes gave her. They were like grass-green drops in its round head, shining and deep. On top of the green was that milkiness that the eyes of all young creatures have, and she could tell that the puppy was finding it hard to see her. But, somewhere in the green depths, she had a glimpse of something huge and wonderful which made her feel almost respectful.

"Why not call it Shamus?" Robin suggested. "Then you'd get in first before Basil does."

"That's a silly name," said Kathleen.

"Then you ought to give it a cat sort of name. How about Leo? That means a lion."

"I think lions have yellow eyes," Kathleen said dubiously. "But it's more majestic than Shamus. I'll think about it while I give him his bottle."

She presented Sirius with a rubbery nipple leaking milk. He fastened on it gladly, and Kathleen fed him tenderly— and far too much. Sirius was sick. It did not trouble him particularly, but Kathleen seemed to have a great deal of cleaning up to do. And while she was cleaning up, Sirius became aware of another presence.

This being was large—at least as large as Kathleen and Robin put together—and reminded him, just a little, of the woman called Mrs. Partridge who had ordered the youth to drown him. She had the same certainty that she would get her own way. And she had—Sirius sensed at once—the same dislike of him. He cowered in the corner of the fender, feeling very small and helpless, while a hard, high voice beat the air about him. It was a voice that was at once very cold and full of all sorts of strong emotions.

". . . bringing this filthy little animal into my house without so much as a by-your-leave . . . not a scrap of consideration for *my* feelings. . . . letting it make a mess all over the hearthrug, and goodness knows what germs it's let loose. And what about the cats? You are a very thoughtless little girl, Kathleen. Lord knows, I've regretted every minute since Harry insisted on foisting you on me, but this is the last *straw!* It's no good sitting there with that mulish look on your face, Kathleen. Robin, take the filthy little beast outside and drown it in the water butt."

"But, Duffie, somebody'd tried to drown him in the river!" Kathleen protested tremulously.

"Whoever it was had more sense than you!" the being called Duffie retorted. "Just look at the mess! Robin, you heard me!"

"I'm clearing the mess up," Kathleen said miserably. "I'll clear up any mess he makes, ever."

"It's because he's only little, Mum," Robin explained. "He didn't know when he'd had enough. But he'll be awfully useful when he grows up. What if burglars get in your shop?"

"There's a perfectly good burglar alarm. For once and for all, I am not having a dirty dog in my house!"

"Please, Duffie, let me keep him," Kathleen pleaded. "I'll

make sure he isn't dirty. He can be for a birthday present.
I haven't had one yet."

This made the owner of the cold voice pause. She gave
a nasty sigh of annoyance that raised the hair along Sirius's
back. "And feed it and buy it a license and walk it and
house-train it! I'd like to see a little sloven like you do all
that! No."

"If you let me keep him," Kathleen said desperately, "I'll
do anything you want. I'll do all the housework and cook
the meals, and everything. I promise."

There was another pause. "Well," said the cold voice. "I
suppose it'll save me— All right. Keep the filthy thing.
But don't blame me if the cats tear it to pieces."

Then the large being was gone and the air was peaceful
again. Sirius found himself being picked up and hugged.

"Careful. You'll make him sick again," said Robin, and
he wandered hastily off, for fear there might be more cleaning up to do.

"You'll be good, won't you? I know you will," Kathleen
whispered to Sirius. Wet drops fell on his head and he
wriggled. "You'll be my very own faithful hound. I know
you're special, because of your eyes. We'll have adventures
together. And don't you mind those cats. I'll see they don't
hurt you." Kathleen put Sirius gently back in his basket
again and he fell asleep.

By the evening, he was recovered enough to scramble out
and go exploring. He went, rocking on his four unsteady
paws, with his fluffy string of a tail whipping backwards
and forwards to keep his balance, in among the feet of the

family. His nose glistened from all the new scents. The cats sat high up on shelves or tables, watching him resentfully. Sirius could feel their annoyance, but he could also feel that they did not dare do anything while the people were there, so he took no notice of them and concentrated on the feet. The children's feet had cloth and rubbery stuff over them. Robin's and Kathleen's were much the same size, but the cloth on Kathleen's was old and frayed. Basil's feet were surprisingly large. While Sirius was sniffing them, Basil leaned down and called him Shamus O'Cat.

"I'm thinking of calling him Leo, really," said Kathleen.

"Rat would be better," said Basil. "Shamus Rat."

"Told you so," said Robin.

There was a new pair of feet present belonging to someone Basil and Robin called Dad, and Kathleen called Uncle Harry. They were the largest feet of all, most interestingly cased in leather, with beautiful strings which came undone when they were bitten. Sirius backed away, his tail whipping, rumbling with delight, a taut shoelace clenched between his teeth.

A voice spoke, more like a clap of thunder than a voice. *"Drop that!"*

Sirius let go at once and meekly went on to the last pair of feet, which were Duffie's. He did not like Duffie, nor the smell of Duffie, but her feet were interesting. The leather on them was only in straps, leaving the ends bare. The ends of both feet divided into a number of stumpy lumps with hard, flat claws on them that looked quite useless. He nosed them wonderingly.

"Get out of it!" said the cold voice.

Sirius obligingly retreated, and—whether it was his dislike of Duffie or simply a call of nature, he did not know—left a puddle between the two sets of toes.

"Oh Leo!" Kathleen plunged down on the spot with a cloth.

"Dirty Shamus Rat!" said Basil.

"That creature—" began Duffie.

The thunderous voice cut in, rumbling peaceably. "Now, now. You've had your say, Duffie. And *I* say a house isn't complete without a dog. What did you say his name was, Kathleen?"

Sirius gathered that he was safe. What the thunderous voice said in this place, the other people obeyed. He went on exploring the room while they argued about what to call him.

The argument was never entirely settled. In the days that followed, Sirius found himself answering to Leo, Shamus, Shamus O'Cat, Shamus Rat, Rat, Dog and That Creature. More names were added as time went on and then dropped. These were the most constant. Basil called him most of them. Duffie called him That Dog or That Creature. Robin usually called him Leo when he was alone with Kathleen, and Shamus if Basil was there. The thunderous voice never called him anything at all. Neither did the cats. Before long, it was only Kathleen who ever called him Leo.

Sirius did not mind. He could tell by the tone of their voices when they meant him, and he answered to that. He liked Kathleen's voice best. It was soft, with a lilt in it which none of the others had, and usually meant he was going to be fed or stroked. Duffie's voice was the one he liked least and, next to hers, Basil's. When Basil called him, it was to flip his nose or roll him painfully about. Even if he did neither of these things, Basil made Sirius feel small and weak, or troubled him by staring jeeringly at his eyes.

His eyes soon lost the milky, puppy look. They became first grass-green, then a lighter, wilder color. "Wolf's eyes," said Basil, and added The Wolf temporarily to the names he called Sirius. About that time, Sirius discovered he could eat from a dish and gave up feeding from a bottle. He grew. And grew. And went on growing.

"Is this thing of yours going to turn out to be a horse?" wondered the thunderous voice, in one of its rare moments of interest.

"A Great Dane perhaps?" Robin suggested.

"Oh, I hope not!" Kathleen said, knowing how much Leo ate already. Sirius realized she was worried and wagged his tail consolingly outside his basket. It was a long, strong tail by this time, and he filled the basket to overflowing.

His tail was a great trial to everyone. He would wag it. He beat dust out of the carpet with it every time one of the household came into the room. He meant it as politeness. In a cloudy part of his mind, which he could never quite find, he knew he was grateful to them—even to Duffie—for feeding and housing him. But only Kathleen and Robin appreciated his courtesy. The rest said, "Must that creature thump like that?" and at other times there was a general outcry.

There were times when that tail seemed to have a life of its own. When he was trotting around the house, Sirius normally carried it arched upward in a crescent and forgot about it. He dimly thought, in that cloudy part of his mind, that he could not always have had a tail, because he never remembered it until it was too late. If the least thing happened to excite him, if Robin started to dance about, or Kathleen came in from shopping, Sirius would bound jovially forward and his tail would go whipping round and round in circles, hitting everything in its path. Ornaments came off low tables and broke. Cats were battered this way and that. Papers flew about. Basil's fossils were scattered. The next thing he knew, a cat was scratching him, or a strong arm was beating him. He was beaten oftener for wagging his tail than he was over house-training. One of the most constant memories he had of those early days was of lying aching and ashamed under the sideboard, while Kathleen, often in tears, cleared up a breakage or another kind of mess. Duffie was always looming above her.

"I warn you, Kathleen. If that creature ever gets into my shop, I shall have it destroyed." Her cold voice was so menacing that Sirius always shivered.

The shop took up the two rooms in the front of the house. Duffie spent most of every day in it, either making odd whirrings and clatterings in the nearest room, or talking to all the people who came in and out in the room farthest away, which opened on the street. These people were mostly women with loud voices, who all called the owner Duffie. If Duffie happened to be in the living room looming over

Kathleen when they came, they would stand and shout, "What-ho, Duffie! It's me!" until Duffie came.

Now, in those days, Sirius's whole world was the house and the yard behind it. The shop left very little of the world downstairs over, so he was naturally curious to see into this shop. He was naturally curious anyway. Kathleen often said, "I know they say *Curiosity killed the cat,* but it ought to be *killed the dog.* Get your nose out, Leo." Sirius made a number of attempts to poke his blunt, inquiring nose around the door that led to the shop. Duffie always stopped him. Mostly she kicked at him with a sandaled foot. Sometimes she hit him with a broom. And once she slammed the door against his nose, which hurt him considerably. But he kept on trying. It was not that the dusty, clayey smell from beyond the door was particularly pleasing, or that he wanted to be with Duffie. It was that he felt he was being cheated of the greater part of his world. Besides, the cats were allowed inside, and he was rapidly becoming very jealous of those cats.

By this time, it would have been hard to say whether the cats were more jealous of Sirius than he of them. He envied the cats their delicacy and disdain, the ease with which they leaped to places far out of his reach and the way they came and went so secretly. He could not go anywhere or do anything without somebody noticing. The cats, on their part, disliked him for being a dog, for being new and for taking up everyone's attention.

They were three rather neglected cats. Until Kathleen came, no one except Duffie had taken any notice of them

at all. Duffie, from time to time, took it into her head that
she loved cats. When this happened, she would seize a struggling cat, hold it against her smock and announce, "Did-
dumsdiddy, Mother loves a pussy then!"

Romulus and Remus, who were twin tabbies, both escaped
from this treatment as soon as they could fight loose. But
Tibbles bore it. She had an affectionate nature, and even
this seemed better to her than total neglect. Tibbles was an
elegant cat, mostly white, with a fine tabby patch on her
back, and worthy of better treatment.

All three welcomed Kathleen with delight. She fed them
generously, knew Romulus and Remus apart from the first,
and gave Tibbles all the affection she wanted. Then Sirius
came. Kathleen still fed the cats generously, but that was all
Sirius would let her do. The day Sirius found Tibbles sitting
on Kathleen's knee was the first time he barked. Yapping in
a furious soprano, he flung himself at Kathleen and managed
to get his front paws almost above her kneecaps. Tibbles
arose and spat. Her paw shot out, once, twice, three times,
before Sirius could remove himself. He was lucky not to
lose an eye. But he continued to bark, and Tibbles, very
ruffled, escaped onto the sideboard, furious and swearing
revenge.

"Oh Leo!" Kathleen said reproachfully. "That's not kind.
Why shouldn't she sit on my knee?"

Sirius did not understand the question, but he was determined that Tibbles should sit on Kathleen's knee only over
his dead body. Kathleen was *his*. The trouble was, he could
not trust Kathleen to remember this. Kathleen was kind to

all living things. She fed birds, rescued mice from the cats, and tried to grow flowers in a row of cracked cups on her bedroom window sill. Sirius slept in Kathleen's bedroom, at first in the basket, then on the end of her bed when the basket grew uncomfortably tight. Kathleen would sit up in bed, with a book open in front of her, and talk to him for hours on end. Sirius could not understand what she was saying, but he darkly suspected she was telling him of her abounding love for all creatures.

One night, when it was spitting with rain, Romulus forgot about Sirius and came in through Kathleen's bedroom window to spend the night on her bed as he had done before Sirius came. That was the first time Sirius really growled. He leaped up rumbling. Romulus growled too and fled helter-skelter, knocking over Kathleen's flower-cups as he went.

"You mustn't, Leo," said Kathleen. "He's *allowed* to. Now look what you've made him do!" She was so miserable about her broken flowers that Sirius had to lick her face.

After that, Sirius knew the cats were putting their heads together to get revenge. He did not care. He knew they were clever, Tibbles especially, but he was not in the least afraid of them. He was at least twice their size by now and still growing. His paws, as Kathleen remarked, were as big as teacups, and he was getting some splendid new teeth. Robin, who was always reading books about dogs, told Kathleen that Leo was certainly half Labrador. But what the other half of him was, neither of them could conjecture. Sirius's unusually glossy coat was a wavy golden-cream, except for the two red-brown patches, foxy red, one over each ear. Then there were those queer green eyes.

"Red Setter, perhaps?" Robin said doubtfully. "He's got those feathery bits at the backs of his legs."

"Mongrel," said Basil. "His father was a white rat and his mother was a fox."

"Vixen," Robin corrected him.

"I thought you'd agree," said Basil.

Kathleen, who seldom argued with Basil, said nothing and went away upstairs to make the beds, with Sirius trotting after. "I think you're really a griffin," she said. "Look." She opened the door of Duffie's wardrobe so that Sirius could see himself in the long mirror.

Sirius did not make the mistake of thinking it was another dog. He did not even go around the back of the mirror to see how his reflection got there. He simply sat himself down and looked, which impressed Kathleen very much. "You *are* intelligent!" she said.

Sirius met his own strange eyes. He had no means of knowing they were unusual, but, all the same, just for a moment, he seemed to be looking at immeasurable distances down inside those eyes. There he saw people and places so different from Duffie's bedroom that they were almost inconceivable. That was only for an instant. After that, they were only the green eyes of a fat curly puppy. Annoyed by something he could not understand, Sirius yawned like a crocodile, showing all his splendid new teeth.

"Come, come!" said Kathleen, laughing. "You're not that boring!"

Those splendid teeth had Sirius in trouble the next day. The urge was on him to chew. And chew and chew. He chewed his basket into a kind of grass skirt. Then he went on to the hearthrug. Kathleen tore the hearthrug out of his mouth and gave him an old shoe, imploring him not to chew anything else but that. Sirius munched it threadbare in a half hour and looked around for something else. Basil had left a box of fossils on the floor. Sirius selected a piece of petrified wood out of it, propped it between his front paws, and was settling down to some glorious gritty grating when Basil found him. Basil kicked him, rolling and howling, across the room.

"Stinking Rat! Do that again and I'll kill you!"

Sirius dared not move. He wagged his tail apologetically and look around for something else to bite on. Nicely within reach trailed a black chewy wire from a shelf above. He had his head up and the wire across the corners of his mouth in an ecstasy of chew, when Robin descended on him and put a stop to that.

"Kathleen! He's eaten the telephone wire now!"

"I'll go and buy a rubber bone," said Kathleen. She went out. Robin, rapidly and furtively, dreading Duffie coming, wrapped black sticky tape around the telephone wire. Basil was anxiously making sure none of his fossils had been eaten. No one attended to Sirius, crouched under the sideboard. He lay there, nose on paws, and there it came to him what it was he really wanted to chew. The ideal thing. With a little ticker-tack of claws, he crept to the door and up the stairs. He nosed open the door of the main bedroom without difficulty and, with a little more trouble, succeeded in opening the wardrobe too. Inside were shoes—long large leather shoes, with laces and thick chewable soles. Sirius selected the juiciest and took it under the bed to enjoy in peace.

The thunderous voice found him there and chased him around the house with a walking stick. Duffie spoke long and coldly. Kathleen wept. Robin tried to explain about teething. Basil jeered. And throughout, Tibbles sat thoughtfully on the sideboard, giving the inside of her left front leg little hasty licks, like a cat seized with an idea. Sirius saw her. To show his contempt and to soothe his feelings, he went into the kitchen and ate the cats' supper. Then he lay down glumly to gnaw the unsatisfactory rubber thing Kathleen had bought him.

"That settles it," said Duffie. "That Creature is not going to spend all day in the house when you go back to school. He's going to be tied up in the yard."

"Yes. Yes, all right," Kathleen said humbly. "I'll take him for walks when I get home. I'll start getting him used to it today."

She had bought something else besides the bone. There was a red jingly strap, which she buckled around Sirius's neck. He did not like it. It was tight and it itched. But, twist as he might, he could not get it off. Then Kathleen hitched another strap with a loop at one end to the red one, and, to his great delight, opened the side door on the outside world, where he had never been before.

Sirius set off down the side of the house in a delighted rush. He was brought up short with a jerk and a jingle.

Something seemed to be pulling his neck. He strained. He dragged. He made hoarse choking noises to show Kathleen what was wrong. He stood on his hind legs to be free.

"No, Leo," said Kathleen. "You mustn't pull."

But he went on pulling. The indignity was too much. He was not a slave, or a prisoner. He was Sirius. He was a free luminary and a high effulgent. He would not be held. He braced his four legs, and Kathleen had to walk backward, towing him.

3 BEING TOWED is hard on the paws, let alone the legs and ears. But Sirius was stiff with shock, and Kathleen had to drag him right down the passage. He was not what he seemed. He felt as if the world had stopped, just in front of his forefeet, and he was looking down into infinite cloudy green depths. What was down in those depths frightened him, because he could not understand it.

"Really, Leo!" said Kathleen, at the end of the passage.

Sirius gave in and began to walk, absently at first, trying to understand what had happened. But he had no leisure to think. As soon as they were in the street, half a million new smells hit his nose simultaneously. Kathleen was walking briskly, and so were other legs around her. Beyond, large groaning things shot by with a swish and a queer smell. Sirius pulled away sideways to have a closer look at those things and was distracted at once by a deliciously rotten something in the gutter. When Kathleen dragged him off that, there were smells several dogs had left on a lamppost, and, beyond that, a savory dustbin, decaying fit to make his mouth water.

"No, Leo," said Kathleen, dragging.

Sirius was forced to follow her. It irked his pride to be so small and weak when he knew he had once been almost infinitely strong. How had he come to be like this? What had happened to reduce him? But he could not think of the answer when something black was trickling on the pavement, demanding to be sniffed all over at once.

"Leave it," said Kathleen. "That's dirty."

It seemed to Sirius that Kathleen said this to everything really interesting. It seemed to Kathleen that she had said it several hundred times before they came to the meadow by the river. And here more new smells imperiously wanted attention. Kathleen took off the leash and Sirius bounded away, jingling and joyful, into the damp green grass. He ranged to and fro, rooting and sniffing, his tail crooked into a stiff and eager question mark. Beautiful. Goluptious scents. What was he looking for in all this glorious green plain? He was looking for something. He became more and more certain of that. This bush? No. This smelly lump, then? No. What then?

There was a scent, beyond, which was vaguely familiar. Perhaps that was what he was looking for. Sirius galloped questing toward it, with Kathleen in desperate pursuit, and skidded to a stop on the bank of the river. He knew it, this whelming brown thing—he dimly remembered—and the hair on his back stood up slightly. This was not what he was looking for. And surely, although it was brown and never for a second stopped crawling past him, by the smell it was only water? Sirius felt he had better test this theory—and quickly. The rate the stuff was crawling, it would soon have crawled right past and away if he did not catch it at once. He descended cautiously to it. Yes, it was water, crawling water. It tasted a good deal more full-bodied than the water Kathleen put down for him in the kitchen.

"Oh, no!" said Kathleen, panting up to find him black-legged and stinking, lapping at the river as if he had drunk nothing for a week. "Come out."

Sirius obligingly came out. He was very happy. He wiped some of the mud off his legs onto Kathleen's and continued his search of the meadow. He still could not think what he was looking for. Then, suddenly, as puppies do, he got exhausted. He was so tired that all he could do was to sit down and stay sitting. Nothing Kathleen said would make him move. So she sat down beside him and waited until he had recovered.

And there, sitting in the center of the green meadow, Sirius remembered a little. He felt as if, inside his head, he was sitting in a green space that was vast, boundless, queer, and even more alive than the meadow in which his body sat. It was appalling. Yet, if he looked around the meadow, he knew that in time he could get to know every tuft and molehill in it. And, in the same way, he thought he might come to know the vaster green spaces inside his head.

I don't understand, he thought, panting, with his tongue hanging out. Why do those queer green spaces seem to be me?

But his brain was not yet big enough to contain those spaces. It tried to close itself away from them. In doing so, it nipped the green vision down to a narrow channel, and urgent and miserable memories poured through. Sirius knew he had been wrongly accused of something. He knew someone had let him down terribly. How and why he could not tell, but he knew he had been condemned. He had raged, and it had been no use. And there was a Zoi. He had no idea what a Zoi was, but he knew he had to find it, urgently. And how could he find it, not knowing what it was like, when he himself was so small and weak that even a well-meaning being like Kathleen could pull him about on the end of a strap? He began whining softly, because it was so hopeless and so difficult to understand.

"There, there." Kathleen gently patted him. "You *are* tired, aren't you? We'd better get back."

She got up from her damp hollow in the grass and fastened the leash to the red collar again. Sirius came when she dragged. He was too tired and dejected to resist. They went back the way they had come, and this time Sirius was not very interested in all the various smells. He had too much else to worry about.

As soon as Robin set eyes on Sirius, he said something. It was, "He's pretty filthy, isn't he?" but of course Sirius could not understand. Basil said something too, and Duffie's

cold voice in the distance said more. Kathleen hastily
fetched cloths and towels and rubbed Sirius down and, all
the while, Duffie talked in the way that made Sirius cower.
He suddenly understood two things. One was that Duffie—
and perhaps the whole family—had power of life and death
over him. The other was that he needed to understand what
they said. If he did not know what Duffie was objecting to,
he might do it again and be put to death for it.

After that he fell asleep on the hearthrug with all four
paws stiffly stretched out, and was dead to the world for
a time. He was greatly in the way. Robin shoved him this
way, Basil that. The thunderous voice made an attempt to
roll him away under the sofa, but it was like trying to roll a
heavy log, and he gave up. Sirius was so fast asleep that he
did not even notice. While he slept, things came a little
clearer in his mind. It was as if his brain was forced larger
by all the things which had been in it that day.

He woke up ravenous. He ate his own supper, and finished what the cats had left of the second supper Kathleen
had given them. He looked around hopefully for more, but
there was no more. He lay sighing, with his face on his great
clumsy paws, watching the family eat their supper—they
always reserved the most interesting food for themselves—
and trying with all his might to understand what they were
saying. He was pleased to find that he had already unwit-
tingly picked up a number of sounds. Some he could even
put meanings to. But most of it sounded like gabble. It took
him some days to sort the gabble into words, and to see
how the words could be put with other words. And when

he had done that, he found that his ears had not been pick-
ing up the most important part of these words.

He thought he had learned the word *walk* straight away.
Whenever Kathleen said it, he sprang up, knowing it meant
a visit to the green meadow and the crawling water. In his
delight at what that word meant, his tail took a life of its
own and knocked things over, and he submitted to being
fastened to the strap because of what came after. But he
thought these pleasures were packed into a noise that went
ork. Basil discovered this, and had great fun with him.

"Pork, Rat!" he would shout. "Stalk! Cork!"

Each time, Sirius sprang up, tail slashing, fox-red drooping ears pricked, only to be disappointed. Basil howled with
laughter.

"No go, Rat. Auk, hawk, fork!"

In fact, Basil did Sirius a favor, because he taught him
to listen to the beginnings of words. By the end of a week,
Sirius was watching for the noise humans made by pouting
their mouth into a small pucker. It looked a difficult noise.
He was not sure he would ever learn to make it himself.
But he now knew that when *ork* began with this sound,
it was real, and not otherwise. He did not respond to *fork*
or *talk* and Basil grew quite peevish about it.

"This Rat's no fun anymore," he grumbled.

Kathleen was relieved that Leo had almost stopped chew-
ing things. Sirius was too busy learning and observing to do
more than munch absently on his rubber bone. He ached
for knowledge now. He kept perceiving a vast green something in himself, which was always escaping from the cor-

ner of his eye. He could never capture it properly, but he saw enough of it to know that he was now something stupid and ignorant, slung on four clumsy legs, with a mind like an amiable sieve. He had to learn why this was, or he would never be able to understand about a Zoi.

So Sirius listened and listened, and watched till his head ached. He watched cats as well as humans. And slowly, slowly, things began to make sense to him. He learned that animals were held to be inferior to humans, because they were less clever, and smaller and clumsier. Humans used their hands in all sorts of devious, delicate ways. If there was something their hands could not do, they were clever enough to think of some tool to use instead. This perception was a great help to Sirius. He had odd, dim memories of himself using a Zoi rather as humans used tools. But animals could not do this. That was how humans had power of life and death over them.

Nevertheless, Sirius watched, fascinated, the way the cats, and Tibbles in particular, used their paws almost as cleverly as humans. Tibbles could push the cover off a meat dish, so that Romulus and Remus could make their claws into hooks and drag out the meat inside. She could pull down the catch of the kitchen window and let herself in at night if it was raining. And she could open any door that did not have a round handle. Sirius would look along his nose to his own great stumpy paws and sigh deeply. They were as useless as Duffie's feet. He might be stronger than all three cats put together, but he could not use his paws as they did. He saw that this put him further under the power of humans than the cats. Because of their skill, the cats lived a busy and private life outside and inside the house, whereas he had to wait for a human to lead him about. He grew very depressed.

Then he discovered he could be clever too.

It was over the smart red jingly collar. Kathleen left it buckled around his neck after the first walk. Sirius hated it. It itched, and its noise annoyed him. But he very soon saw that it was more than an annoyance—it was the sign and tool of the power humans had over him. One of them—Basil for instance—had only to take hold of it to make him a helpless prisoner. If Basil then flipped his nose or took his bone away, it was a sign of the power he felt he had.

So Sirius set to work to make sure he could be free of that collar when he wanted. He scratched. And he scratched. And scratched. Jingle, jingle, jingle went the collar.

"Make that filthy creature stop scratching," said Duffie.

"I think his collar may be on too tight," said Robin. He and Kathleen examined it and decided to let it out two holes.

This was a considerable relief to Sirius. The collar no longer itched, though in its looser state it jingled more annoyingly than before. That night, after a little maneuvering under Kathleen's bed, he managed to hook it to one of Kathleen's bedsprings and tried to pull it off by walking away backwards. The collar stuck behind his ears. It hurt. It would not move. He could not get it off and he could not get it on again. He could not even get it off the bedspring. His ears were killing him. He panicked, yelping and jumping till the bed heaved.

Kathleen sat up with a shriek. "Leo! Help! There's a ghost under my bed!" Then she added, much more reasonably, "What on earth are you *doing,* Leo?" After that, she switched on the light and came and looked. "You silly little dog! How did you get into that pickle? Hold still now." She unhooked Sirius and dragged him out from under the bed. He was extremely grateful and licked her face hugely. "Give over," said Kathleen. "And let's get some sleep."

Sirius obediently curled up on her bed until she was asleep again. Then he got down and started scratching once more. Whenever no one was near, he scratched diligently, always in the same place, on the loops of loose skin under his chin. It did not hurt much there and yet, shortly, he had made himself a very satisfactory raw spot.

"Your horse has its collar on too tight," the thunderous voice told Kathleen. "Look."

Kathleen looked, and felt terrible. "Oh, my poor Leo!" She let the collar out three more holes.

That night, to his great satisfaction, Sirius found he could leave the collar hanging on the bedspring, while he ambled around the house with only the quiet ticker-tack of his claws to mark his progress. It was not quite such an easy matter to get the collar on again. Kathleen woke twice more thinking there was a ghost under her bed, before Sirius thought of pushing his head into the collar from the other side. Then it came off the bedspring and onto his neck in one neat movement. He curled up on Kathleen's bed feeling very pleased with himself.

This piece of cunning made Sirius much more confident. He began to suspect that he could settle most difficulties if he thought about them. His body might be clumsy, but his mind was quite as good as any cat's. It was fortunate he realized this, because one afternoon when Kathleen, Robin and Basil were all out, long before Sirius had learned more than a few words of human speech, Tibbles did her best to get rid of him for good.

Sirius, bored and lonely, drew himself quietly up onto the sofa and fell gingerly asleep there. He liked that sofa. He considered it unfair of the humans that they insisted on keeping all the most comfortable places for themselves. But he did not dare do more than doze. Duffie was moving about upstairs. It seemed to be one of the afternoons when she did not shut herself away in the shop and, Sirius had learned by painful experience, you had to be extra wary on those days.

He had been dozing there for nearly an hour, when Romulus jumped on him. He hit Sirius like a bomb, every claw out and spitting abuse. Sirius sprang up with a yelp. He was more surprised than anything at first. But Romulus was fat and determined. He dug his claws in and stuck to Sirius's back and Sirius, for a second or so, could not shake him off. In those seconds, Sirius became furiously angry. It was like a sheet of green flame in his head. How dared Romulus! He hurled the cat off and went for him, snarling and showing every pointed white tooth he had. Romulus took one look. Then he flashed over the sofa arm and vanished. Sirius's teeth snapped on empty air. By the time he reached the carpet, Romulus was nowhere to be seen.

A bubbling hiss drew Sirius's attention to Remus, crouched in the open doorway to the shop. Remus bared his teeth and spat. At that, Sirius's rage flared vaster and greener still. He responded with a deep rumbling growl that surprised him nearly as much as it surprised Remus. A great ridge of fur came up over his back and shoulders and his eyes blazed green. Remus stared at this nightmare of eyes, teeth and bristle, and his own fur stood and stood and stood, until he was nearly twice his normal size. He spat. Sirius throbbed like a motorcycle and crept forward, slow and stiff-legged, to tear Remus to pieces. He was angry, angry, angry.

Remus only waited to make sure Sirius was indeed coming his way. Then he bolted without courage or dignity. He had done what his mother wanted, but not even for Tibbles was he going to face this nightmare a second longer than he had to. When Sirius reached the door of the shop, there was no sign of Remus. There was only Tibbles, alone in the middle of a dusty floor.

Sirius stopped when his face was around the door. In spite of his rage, he knew something was not right here. This door should have been shut. Tibbles must have opened it. She must be trying to tempt him inside for reasons of her own. The prudent thing would be not to be tempted. But he had always wanted to explore the shop, and he was still very angry. To see what would happen, he pushed the door further open and let out another great throbbing growl at Tibbles.

At the sight and sound of him, Tibbles became a paper-thin archway of a cat, and her tail stood above in a desperate question mark. Was this a puppy or a monster? She was terrified. But she stood her ground because this was her chance to get rid of it.

Her terror gave Sirius rather an amusing sense of power. Slow and stiff-legged, he strutted into the room. Tibbles spat and drifted away sideways, so arched that she looked like a piece of paper blowing in the wind. Sirius saw she wanted him to chase her. Just for a moment, he did wonder how it would feel to take her arched and narrow back between his teeth and shake his head till she snapped, but he was sure she would jump out of reach somewhere before he could catch her. So he ignored her. Instead, he swaggered across the dusty floor to look at the objects piled by the walls and stacked on the shelves.

He sniffed them cautiously. What were these things? As curiosity gained the upper hand in him, his growl died away and the hair on his back settled down into glossy waves again. The things had a blank, muddy smell. Some were damp and pink, some pale and dry, some again shiny and painted in ugly gray-greens. They were something like the cups humans drank out of, and he thought they might be made of the same stuff as the dish labeled DOG in which Kathleen gave him his water. But Sirius could not have got his tongue into most of them. No human could have drunk out of any. Then he remembered the thing on the living-room mantelpiece Kathleen had smashed that morning when she was dusting. It had held one rose. Duffie had been furious.

Sirius understood now. These things were rose-holders and they broke. Let a dog chase a cat among them and the result would be spectacular. Duffie would certainly carry out all her cold threats. It was clever of Tibbles.

Cautiously, carefully, walking stiff-legged in order not to knock anything, Sirius explored the two rooms thoroughly. He sniffed at rows of hand-thrown pottery. He nosed glaze. He investigated damp new clay. He put his feet on a stool to examine the pink and dusty wheel on which Duffie made the things, and snuffed at the oven where she fired them. That was a better smell than most. It brought a queer tinge of homesickness. He went into the shop itself, where rows of shiny pots in dull colors waited for people to buy them. He did not find it very interesting. In fact, the whole place was rather a disappointment. It astonished him that even Duffie could find things like this important. But he was sure she did. The cold dusty smell of the place matched her personality.

Tibbles followed him about like a drifting outraged shadow. How could the creature resist chasing her to go sniffing about like this? But Sirius took no notice of her at all. When he had seen enough, he turned carefully and carefully pit-patted toward the open door. He was going back to the sofa.

It was too much for Tibbles. Determined to carry out her plan, she dashed at Sirius and clawed his face. Then she leaped for a high shelf in the place where pottery was stacked thickest.

That was her undoing. She was in too much of a hurry to judge her jump properly, or perhaps she was simply confident that Sirius would be blamed for anything that broke. She missed the space she was aiming for and collided with a mighty purple vase. Slowly and imposingly, the vase tipped over, knocked Tibbles sideways and fell into a heap of pots beneath. Tibbles just managed to hook her claws into the very end of the shelf, where she hung, scrabbling underneath the shelf for a foothold. Sirius bolted, with the smash ringing in his ears. He had a last sight of Tibbles desperately hanging and scrabbling, and the other end of the shelf tipping sharply upward.

4 SIRIUS SHOT soundlessly across the living-room carpet. His hind legs were instinctively lowered and his tail wrapped under them. Duffie was pounding downstairs. From the shop came smash after crash after smash. Pots were sliding down the sloping shelf, over the helpless Tibbles, and breaking one upon another in a heap by the doorway. As Duffie burst into the living room, Sirius shot into the kitchen, shot across it to the space under the sink and crammed himself in behind the waste bucket.

Romulus was hiding there too. He spat half-heartedly at Sirius, but both of them knew the situation was too serious for fighting. They both crouched, trembling, packed side by side into the slimy space, listening to the dreadful noises from the shop.

In the heat of the moment, Sirius and Romulus found they were communicating with one another.

"What happened? What went wrong?"

"It was her fault. She jumped on a shelf. Everything fell off it."

"She's being killed. *Do* something!"

"*You* do something."

It certainly sounded as if Tibbles were being killed. There was more heavy crashing, and cold high yelling from Duffie. After that came a dreadful screech, half cat, half human. Remus shot into the kitchen, a fat stripy streak of panic, and made for the waste pail too. When he saw Sirius and Romulus already there, he stopped, looped into a frenzy, glaring.

"Help! Let me hide! She's killing us!"

Duffie was now raving around the living room. "Where's that *flaming* CAT?"

At the sound, Remus somehow packed himself in beside Romulus, quivering as if there was a motor beside him. Sirius found himself being oozed out on the other side. "Hey!"

"Sorry, sorry, sorry!" shivered Remus. "Oh, ye gods!"

There was a scream like a steam siren from the next room. Something crashed, probably the new rose-holder.

"Damn!" yelled Duffie. *"Got you, you fiend!"* It was clear Tibbles had been caught. A heavy, sharp thumping began. It was as strong and regular as the noise Kathleen had made when she hung the carpets on the clothesline and beat them with a beater. Duffie yelled, in time with the thumps, "I'll—teach—you—to—break—my—pottery!"

Sirius found he could not have this. Whatever Tibbles deserved, it was not being beaten to death. His dog's hatred of strife in his family fetched him out from under the sink. That, and a strong green sense of justice, sent him scampering to the living room, followed by a gust of amazement from Remus and Romulus.

Duffie had her sandals planted wide apart on the hearthrug. She had Tibbles dangling wretchedly from one hand, curled as stiff and small as possible, while her other hand clouted away at Tibbles, hard and rhythmically. At the sight, Sirius's sense of justice became mixed with anger. He would dearly have liked to plant his jawful of white teeth in the bulging muscle of Duffie's calf. He had to tell himself she would taste nasty, he wanted to bite her so much. He launched himself at Duffie instead, and managed to land hard against her stomach before he fell on the floor. Duffie staggered.

"Drat you, animal! Get away!"

Sirius got up and began to leap about Duffie, reaching for Tibbles and barking excitedly.

"Will you stop interfering!" Duffie shouted, lashing out with a sandal.

Sirius knew he was not big enough to reach Tibbles.

Duffie was holding her dangling high out of reach. But he ran in a swift figure of eight around her feet as she kicked out, and made her overbalance. Duffie loosened her hold on Tibbles in order to catch at the mantelpiece. Tibbles dropped with a thump on all four feet and was off like a white flash upstairs.

"Damn!" shrieked Duffie, and lunged at Sirius. He ran away around the sofa, expecting to be beaten with a broom again.

Luckily, they had only been twice around the sofa when the side door opened and Robin, Basil and Kathleen trooped in.

"What's going on?" said Basil.

To the surprise and relief of Sirius, Duffie forgot about him and began to rage long and shrilly about the damage those wretched cats had done in the shop. While the side door was open, Romulus and Remus seized their chance and fled through it. Neither of them reappeared again that day. Sirius supposed it would have been prudent of him to do the same, but he was not really tempted. He was too glad to see Kathleen again. He jumped up against her and squeaked with pleasure.

While Duffie was busy dramatically throwing open the shop door and pointing to the heap of smithereens inside, Kathleen wrapped her arms around Sirius. "I'm glad it wasn't you for once," she whispered.

It seemed unfair to Sirius that it should be Kathleen who cleared up the broken pottery. But he had noticed that

Kathleen always did do an unfair amount of work. He lay and whined in protest outside the shop door, until she had finished and was able to take him to the meadow. Duffie, meanwhile, stumped away upstairs to find Tibbles. But Tibbles had hidden herself cunningly in the very back of the linen closet and Duffie did not find her.

After supper that evening, Duffie angrily shut herself in the shop and worked away at her potter's wheel to replace some of the breakages. When she heard the wheel whirring, Tibbles dared at last to emerge. Very sore and ruffled and hungry, she limped downstairs and into the living room. Only Sirius saw her. Robin, Kathleen, Basil and the thunderous voice were all crowded around the table over some kind of game. Sirius was on the hearthrug with a tough raw bone propped between his paws and his head laid sideways, grating deliciously with his back teeth. He looked at Tibbles across his nose. Tibbles stopped short in the doorway, seeing him looking.

"It's all right. It's quite safe," Sirius told her. "She's in the shop. And there's a whole lot of scraps still down in the kitchen."

Tibbles did not reply. She stepped off delicately to the kitchen, shaking each front paw with a ladylike shudder before she put it down. Sirius, in a dog's equivalent of a shrug, went back to his bone.

Quite a while later, when Sirius had done with the bone and was snoozing, Tibbles limped out of the kitchen and came slowly over to the hearthrug. Though she looked rather less wretched, she was still very ruffled. She sat down, wrapped her tail across her front feet and stared fixedly at Sirius.

"I still hurt. It's all your fault."

Sirius raised an eyebrow and rolled one green eye up at her. "It was your fault, too. But I'm sorry. I was afraid she was going to kill you."

"She was," said Tibbles. "She loves those silly mud pots. Thank you for stopping her." She raised a front paw and licked it half-heartedly. "I feel awful," she said miserably. "What can I do?"

"Come over here and I'll lick you," Sirius suggested, greatly daring.

He expected Tibbles to treat the suggestion with contempt, but, instead, she got up and, casually, as if she did not care particularly, she settled down between his front paws. Most astonished and very flattered, Sirius gingerly licked her back. She tasted clean and fluffy.

"Farther up and over to the right," Tibbles said, tucking her paws under her gracefully.

Half an hour later, Kathleen looked up from the cards. "Goodness gracious!" she exclaimed. "Just look at that now!"

Everybody looked, and exclaimed to see Tibbles tucked up like a tuffet between the forepaws of the dog with the dog's head resting against her. Tibbles had flat wet patches all over the tabby part of her back from being licked. When she saw them looking, she raised her head and stared at them defiantly. "And why shouldn't I sit here?" Then she turned her pink nose gently to Sirius's black one and settled down to purring again.

Sirius's heavy tail flapped on the carpet. He felt warm and proud to have this lovely white cat purring against him. He looked down at her small humped shape and wondered. It was familiar. So, in a dim back-to-front way, was everything that had happened that afternoon. Some time, in a misty green past, there had been a time with three other beings when he had flown into a rage, only then, as far as he could remember, the disaster had been his and not his Companion's.

Then he remembered, and with great sadness. Once, somewhere else, he had had a Companion, as small and white and nearly as elegant as Tibbles. He had loved this Companion with all his heart, and given her anything she wanted. Then he had been forced to leave her. He could not remember why, but remembering just that was bad enough. He was glad Tibbles was there to make up for it a little. And Kathleen. Sirius cast an eye up at Kathleen, sighing. He had Kathleen and now Tibbles. Perhaps he should not be sad after all. But deep down inside him there was such green misery that he could have cried, if dogs could cry.

That night Tibbles came and curled up on Kathleen's bed beside Sirius. "You're heavy, the two of you," Kathleen said, heaving them about with her feet. "If you weren't so warm, I'd kick you off." She managed to find a space for her feet along beside the wall and fell asleep murmuring, "I'm glad you like one another. But what about poor old Romulus and Remus?"

However, to Kathleen's pleasure, her puppy now got on well with all three cats. Romulus and Remus were not as affectionate to Sirius as Tibbles, but that was because it was not in their nature. But they liked him. They respected him for rescuing Tibbles when neither of them would have dared. And he was big enough to warm a number of cats at once. It became quite a regular thing—as soon as the cats had ceased keeping out of Duffie's way—to find all four animals piled together in a heap on the hearthrug, the cats purring and Sirius lazily thumping his tail. Sirius liked this heap. It reminded him of the time when he had wriggled in a crowd of other puppies. He became very fond of all three cats. They were quaint and knowing. It made him feel cleverer to be friends with them, and it made him feel very clever indeed when he discovered that they could not understand what humans said.

Before long, Sirius was understanding most of human talk. The cats could never learn more than a word or two. They came to depend on Sirius to tell them if anything important was being said. Whenever Duffie went into one of her cold rages, they would come and ask Sirius anxiously what had annoyed her this time. It gave him a pleasant sense of superiority to be able to tell them, even if what he had to say was, "I put mud on the sofa," or "Kathleen gave me a bone when there was still some meat on it."

"It's a pity," Tibbles remarked once, reflectively licking

a paw, "that *she* hates you so much. Perhaps you ought to go and live somewhere else."

"I don't think Kathleen would like me to go," Sirius said.

"Kathleen could go with you. *She* hates her, too," Tibbles observed.

Sirius knew that. One of the first things he tried to find out, as soon as he understood enough talk, was why Duffie hated Kathleen so. It was not easy to discover, because there were so many things connected with it that he did not quite understand. He had to find out why Basil was always jeering at Kathleen for being Irish, and what it meant to be Irish, and why Kathleen spoke in a clipped, lilting way which was different from the rest of the family. Then, one night, Sirius heard a man talking on television in the same rapid but singing accent. Up to then, he had not realized he could learn anything either from the television or the radio. He tried to attend to both after that. The radio defeated him. It spoke in a blank, boxy voice, and it had no face or picture to show him what it was talking about, but the television proved easy to follow and much more informative. At length, he had it all sorted out.

The family was English, and they were called Duffield, but Kathleen was from a country called Ireland, where bad things were happening, and her name was Kathleen O'Brien. In some parts of Ireland, Sirius gathered, cars and buildings were sent up in flames, and people were killed by other people when they answered a knock at their front door. Sometimes the Irish people came and did this in England, too, which accounted for some of the things Basil said.

Kathleen's mother was some kind of relative to Mr. Duffield—he of the thunderous voice—but she had left Ireland when the trouble started and run away to America. And Kathleen's father had been put in prison for taking part in the violence. So Mr. Duffield had sent for Kathleen to come and live with them.

Try as he might, Sirius could not connect Kathleen with the scenes of violence he saw on television. She was the gentlest and most reliable person in the household. But it was plain that both Basil and Duffie did.

Duffie's real name was Daphne Duffield, and she disliked Kathleen for a number of reasons. She had been very angry that Mr. Duffield had not consulted her before sending for Kathleen. That started it. Then Kathleen had no money, except a very little her father had once sent her from prison. Duffie went on at great length, whenever she was cross—which was frequently—about having another mouth to feed, and the cost of clothes, and the cost of Sirius, and the cost of all the china Kathleen broke washing dishes, and a great many other costs. And Duffie disliked Irish people. She called them feckless. She called Kathleen lazy and stupid and sluttish.

Kathleen did all the cooking and most of the housework and dozens of odd jobs as well. But because she was not much older than Robin, she did not always do these things well. Some things she had never done before, some she was not strong enough to do, and sometimes she would start playing with Sirius and forget that she was supposed to be cleaning out the bathroom. Then Duffie came and said all these things, cold and high, making Kathleen tremble and Sirius cower.

Duffie always concluded her scolding with, "And I shall have that creature destroyed unless you mend your ways."

Sirius learned that he was being used to blackmail Kathleen into doing all the work and being scolded into the bargain. When Kathleen had brought him home as a tiny sopping puppy and Duffie had been so very angry, Kathleen had promised to help in the house if Duffie let her keep Sirius. Duffie held her to it. By the end of the summer, Duffie was doing nothing but make pots and scold Kathleen. And Sirius began to long to sink his teeth in Duffie. When she grew cold and shrill at Kathleen, Sirius would eye her bulging calves and yearn with a great yearning to plant a bite in one. He did not do it, because he knew it would not help Kathleen at all. Instead, he rumbled deep in his chest and shook all over with the effort of not biting Duffie. He wished Mr. Duffield would stop Duffie treating Kathleen so badly, but he soon learned that Mr. Duffield was only interested in the work that took him out of the house every day till evening and only complained if Duffie made him uncomfortable. Duffie was not usually unpleasant to Kathleen in the evenings.

Basil was unpleasant to Kathleen most of the time. Sirius soon gathered that Basil did not really dislike Kathleen. He was just imitating Duffie. As Sirius grew larger, and larger still, Basil ceased to frighten him at all. Whenever he saw that Basil's mindless jeering was getting on Kathleen's nerves, Sirius stopped him. Usually it was only necessary to distract Basil by starting a game. But if Basil was being very bad-tempered, Sirius found he could shut him up by staring at him. If he fixed his queer green eyes on Basil's light blue ones and glared, Basil would round on him and jeer at him instead.

"Shamus Wolf! Sneaking filthy mongrel! Rat red-ears!" Sirius never minded this at all.

"I read in a book that no animal could look a human in the eyes," Robin once remarked unwisely.

"Leo's unusual," said Kathleen.

Basil punched Robin's nose. He was about to go on and punch Robin everywhere else, but Sirius rose, rumbling all over, and pushed in between them. Robin ran away and locked himself in the broom closet. Basil was frightened. He saw he could easily turn Shamus Wolf into a permanent enemy, and that would be a waste, since he was far more fun than the stupid cats.

"I'll take the Rat for his walk, if you like," he offered. The Rat was only too ready to come. And, as Kathleen was busy trying to scrape dozens and dozens of tiny new potatoes, she agreed.

So Basil and Sirius went and raced round and round the green meadow, shouting and barking vehemently. They met four other dogs and five other boys, and all of them ran up and down in the mud at the edge of the river until they were both black and weary. When they came home, Robin was waiting, rather puffy-eyed, to fling his arms around Sirius and get licked. Sirius licked him tenderly. He was fond of Robin and knew his position was a difficult one.

Robin was the only one in the family who liked Kathleen, and he adored dogs. But he was only a little boy. He was scared of Basil and he wanted to please Duffie.

Unfortunately, Sirius had forgotten how muddy he was. Mud went on Robin and got plastered on the kitchen floor as well. Duffie came in and coldly raged. Kathleen was in the middle of cooking supper, but she had to find time to get Robin clean clothes and wash the kitchen floor, while Basil jeered and Robin wavered miserably between jeering too and offering to help. It was one of many times when Sirius felt he would be doing Kathleen a kindness if he ran away.

He did not run away because, as he had told Tibbles, he knew it would make Kathleen unhappy. Besides, there were times when Duffie was safely in her shop when he had great fun. Robin, Kathleen—and Basil too, if he was in the mood —would do a romp-thing in the living room, of which the aim seemed to be to stuff Sirius under the sofa—only they usually lost sight of the aim and ended simply rolling in a heap. Or they would all go out to the meadow and throw sticks for Sirius to fetch out of the river. Sirius fetched the stick, but the rule was that he would not bring it to be thrown again. They had to catch him first. He was an expert at dodging. He would wait, with the fringed elbows of his forelegs almost on the ground and the stick temptingly in his mouth, until all three children were almost upon him and putting out their hands to seize the stick. Then he would bounce between them and be away to the other end of the meadow before they could move.

The very best times were when Kathleen and Sirius, not

to speak of Tibbles, had gone to bed in Kathleen's room. Nobody went to sleep for at least an hour. First Kathleen and Sirius had a silly game in which they went very quickly around and around Kathleen's bed. Kathleen tried to crawl and keep her face hidden at the same time, laughing and laughing, while Sirius plowed rapidly after her, trying to lick her face and giving out panting grunts, which were his way of laughing. They played this most nights until Tibbles had had enough and boxed Sirius's ears. Then Kathleen would settle down with a book and talk. She liked reading aloud, so she read to Sirius. Sometimes she explained the book as she read it. Sometimes she just talked. As Sirius understood more and more human talk, he learned a great deal from this—more than he learned from watching television. Tibbles would sit, placid and queenly, washing herself, until she sensed something was interesting Sirius particularly. Then she would ask for an explanation. The odd thing was that, in her own way, Tibbles often knew more than Kathleen.

One night, Kathleen was reading a book of fairy stories. "They're fine stories," she explained to Sirius, "but they're not true. Mind you don't go believing them now."

Sirius liked the stories too, but he was not sure Kathleen was right. He had a notion some of them had more truth in them than Kathleen thought.

Kathleen said suddenly, "Oh, listen to this, Leo!" and she read, *"Of all the hounds he had seen in the world, he had seen no dogs the color of these. The color that was on them was a brilliant shining white, and their ears red; and as the exceeding whiteness of the dogs glittered, so glittered the exceeding redness of their ears.* Fancy that, Leo!" Kathleen said. "They must have looked almost like you. Your coat is sort of shining sometimes, and your ears are nearly red. They were magic dogs, Leo. They belonged to Arawn—he was king in the Underworld. I wonder if you're some relation. It doesn't say anything about the color of their eyes, though." Kathleen leafed on through the story to see if there was any more about the dogs.

"What was that about?" Tibbles asked. Sirius told her. He was excited and puzzled. As far as he knew, his green thoughts came from nothing like an Underworld. And yet Kathleen was right. The description did fit him. "Yes," Tibbles said thoughtfully. "They are a bit like you, I suppose. But they're whiter and their eyes are yellow."

"You mean—these stories are true?" Sirius asked her.

"I don't know," Tibbles said. "I'm talking about nowadays. I've no idea what it was like when the place was full of kings and princesses and magicians and things. Maybe some of the things she reads you could have happened then."

"Don't they happen nowadays?" said Sirius.

"I didn't say that." Tibbles got up irritably and stretched. Stretching, with Tibbles, was an elegant and lengthy business. It began with a long arching of the back, followed by the lowering of her front legs to stretch her shoulders, and finished with a slow further lowering of the back to get the kinks out of each back leg separately. Sirius had to wait till she had finished and curled up again. Then she said, "The trouble with humans is that it's all or nothing with them. They seem to think anything impossible could happen in the old days. And just because these are new days, they tell you none of it is true. Now I'm going to sleep."

5

SOON AFTER THIS, Kathleen had to spend most of every day at school. School, Sirius discovered, was a place where she learned things. He thought this was absurd. Kathleen did not need to learn anything. She was the wisest person he knew. Basil and Robin had to go to school too, which was not so absurd, but they had to dress up in special gray clothes with red stripes around the edges in order to go. Kathleen went in her usual, shabby clothes. Sirius learned that this was because she went to the ordinary school nearby, whereas Basil and Robin went to a school on the other side of the town which charged money for taking them. Duffie earned the money by making and selling those mud pots, but of course she would not spare any money to send Kathleen too. Because Kathleen's school was nearby, she was usually home first, which suited Sirius very well. And he remembered dimly that this had been the way of things before, when he was very tiny and still being fed from a bottle.

This time there was a melancholy difference. Duffie insisted that That Creature be tied up in the yard while Kathleen was away. "I'm not going to have it wandering round the house eating and damaging things all day," she said. "If you *must* keep a dog, you must take the consequences."

"I'm sorry, Leo," Kathleen said, as she led him into the yard and fixed the leash to his collar. She tied the lead to some rope and tied the other end of the rope to the iron bracket that held the clothesline. She fumbled and did it all very slowly. "There," she said at last. "That should be long enough for you. Poor Leo. You're a proper prisoner now." She came back to Sirius and flung her arms around him. "Don't worry. I'll take you for a walk as soon as I get home." Sirius saw she was crying. He was surprised, because these days Kathleen rarely cried. He tried to lick her hands consolingly, but she had to hurry away.

Thereafter, Sirius was taken out every weekday, rain or shine, and tied up in the yard. He disliked rain. It made him itch and shiver. Robin and Kathleen spent all the first weekend of term trying to build him a shelter out of wood, under the bracket in the wall. When Duffie saw it, she was very sarcastic.

"Dogs aren't hurt by a little weather," she said. "What do you pamper it so for?"

"The Rat's used to being in the house, you see," Robin explained.

"You're a little toady, Robin," said Duffie.

The first time Sirius went into the shelter, it fell down on him. He came bolting out of it, with his hind legs lowered against the shower of falling boards and his tail wrapped under his legs. Basil leaned against the house and shrieked with laughter.

"The look on that Rat's face!" he said. "Trust you two! You don't know one end of a nail from the other."

"I'd like to see you do it better," said Robin.

"Right," said Basil. He rebuilt the shelter the next weekend. He did not do it too badly. The shelter stood rather sideways and swayed a little in the wind, but it stayed up. After a day or so, Sirius even dared use it. And before it really fell down again, Mr. Duffield took pity on them and built it yet again, this time properly. Except when the wind was in the east, it was snug.

But the worst thing about being a prisoner in the yard was the long, long hours of boredom. Sirius lay with his head on his paws, sighing heavily, wistfully watching the cats trotting along the walls on their private business, or staring at the gate in the wall of the yard and wishing he could open it. The gate had two bolts, one at the bottom and one about a foot from the top, and a rusty latch in the middle. There was no way that Sirius could see of getting it open.

The cats understood how dreary it was for him. When they had no pressing business elsewhere, Romulus and Remus would kindly sit on the walls of the yard to keep him company. Tibbles frequently shared his shelter. But none of them, not even Tibbles, could help him open that gate.

"Yes, I can undo bolts," Tibbles said. "But those are

rusty and I can't reach the one at the top from the wall. And I can't reach the latch from anywhere. Make Kathleen undo it for you."

But Sirius could not make Kathleen undo the door, because he could not talk to her. It was the bitterest disappointment of his life, and it made his imprisonment even harder to bear. He had never had any doubt that, when he had learned to understand human talk, he would be able to speak it, too. But he could not. Try as he might, he just could not make the proper noises. His throat and his tongue and his jaws were simply the wrong shape. He did not give up easily. He lay in the yard and practiced. But after hours of trying, the most he could manage, by opening his mouth wide, wide, and flapping his tongue, and letting out a sort of tenor groan, was a noise a little like "Hallo."

Kathleen at least understood that. "Listen!" she said. "He's saying Hallo!"

"No he's not," said Basil. "He's just yawning."

"He's not. He's saying Hallo," Kathleen insisted. "He's talking."

"If he's talking, why doesn't he say other things then?" Basil demanded.

"Because he can't. His mouth and things are the wrong shape," Kathleen explained. "But he would if he could. He's very exceptional."

It was a small crumb of comfort to Sirius to know Kathleen understood that much, even if she understood so little else. She could not understand the way he communicated with the cats. It was talk or nothing with humans, it seemed.

Sirius would have given a great deal to have been able to reply just once to some of the interesting things Kathleen said. He would have given a great deal more to be able to tell her that he had to get out of the yard, go away, look for something, to ask her if she knew what a Zoi was, but he could not.

He nosed and hinted and shoved her into the yard. He took her over to the gate and scrabbled at it, whining.

"No, Leo," Kathleen said. "I'm sorry. Duffie would be furious."

So that was that. Week after week, Sirius lay mournfully in the yard, growing bigger and glossier and ever more bored. He despaired of ever getting out. Meanwhile, the weather became colder. In the meadow, the grass was yellow here and there, and the leaves turned brown and blew off the trees. Sometimes the whole field was silvered with little spider webs that got up his nose and made him sneeze, and everywhere smelled of fungus. It began to be dark sooner. Suddenly everyone altered all the clocks and confused Sirius utterly, because he still got hungry at the same time, and Kathleen was not even home from school by then.

That was his blackest week. On its second day, Kathleen had to go out again the moment she came home from school, because there was no sugar. Duffie sent Kathleen to try every shop she could before they all shut. Sirius remained tied up in the yard, puzzled and unhappy, until long after sunset. He had never seen night fall before. He watched the red sun flaring down behind the roofs, leaving an orange stain behind it and a much darker blue sky. After a while, the sky was nearly black. And the stars came out. Wheeling overhead they came, tiny disks of white, green and orange, pinpricks of bluish white, cold tingly red blobs, large orbs, small orbs, more and more, crowding and clustering away into the dark, while behind them wheeled the spangled smear of the Milky Way. Sirius stared upward, dumbfounded. This was home. He should have been there, not tied up in a yard on the edge of things. They were his. And they were so far away. He had no way of reaching them.

He was filled with a vast green sense of loss. Out there, invisible, his lost Companion must be. She was probably too far away to hear. All the same, he threw up his head and howled. And howled. And howled.

"One of you shut that creature up," said Duffie.

Basil came out into the yard and hit Sirius a ringing slap on the muzzle. It hurt, and the echo inside his head nearly deafened Sirius. He put his face down on his paws with a groan.

"Now shut up!" said Basil.

When the door of the house shut, the sense of loss overwhelmed Sirius again. He looked up, and there were the stars, still unattainable. Howls broke out of him again without his being able to stop them. He howled and howled.

"I'll do it," said Robin. He went out and untied Sirius and brought him indoors. It was small and yellow inside, and Sirius began to feel better. "He was miserable," Robin explained to Duffie.

"You spoil that creature so, it's no wonder it thinks it owns the house," said Duffie.

Sirius did not feel truly comfortable until Kathleen came back. And, after that, whenever he saw the stars, he was miserable. Then came a night when the humans seemed to try to imitate stars. There were bangs and fires and star-shapes soaring against the sky. Kathleen made haste to get Sirius indoors, and she seemed so excited that he thought for a while that the Irish people had come with guns to take Kathleen home. He did not want to let her out of his sight.

"No, you have to stay in. It's Guy Fawkes," said Kathleen. "You won't like it anyway."

She was wrong. Sirius was fascinated. It was like being home again. He watched as much as he could see from Kathleen's bed, with his paws propped among the plants on her window sill. The cats could not understand him. They all retired into the linen closet and refused to come out until midnight. Sirius learned from their grumbles that people only had these lovely fires one night in every year. He would have to wait longer than he had lived in order to see them again. The last fire he saw was a great green rocket, exploding far above the houses, spreading like a bright, drifting tree, and turning to nothing while it hung in the sky.

It fascinated Sirius, and worried him, too. He thought about it next day as he lay in the yard along a bar of sunlight. The green fire put him in mind of the vast green something inside him. It hung, drifting, behind the warm and stupid dog thoughts, and he was becoming seriously afraid that if he did not try to understand it and make it a proper part of him, it would drift into nothing like the fire from the rocket. But, however hard he tried, he could not seem to make his dog's brain grasp the green thing, any more than he could make his dog's mouth say words. The green drifted away out of sight, and he found he was falling asleep.

"Effulgency," said someone, "I'm sorry I haven't got round to speaking to you before. I've had a lot to do."

Effulgency? What was this? It was a long time since anyone had addressed Sirius with this kind of respect. Its effect was to bring the green fires he thought he had lost tumbling into his head in such huge bright profusion that he could only lie where he was in the bar of sun, in a sort of emerald daze.

"I have got the right dog, haven't I?" said the voice.

Sirius got over his shock a little and opened his eyes, very blank and green against the sun, to see who was speaking.

"Yes, I have," said the voice.

"I can't see you," Sirius said, frowning into the sunlight. "Who are you?"

The voice gave a little chuckle, fierce and gay. "Yes you can. Don't you remember anything at all?"

That particular fierce, gay sound stirred memories in Sirius. He was surprised to find they were dog memories. But they were so mixed up with vast green things that he was very confused. "You talked to me once before," he said slowly, "when I was drowning in the river. And I think you helped me. That was good of you." He was sure this was not all. Puzzled, he searched the great green spaces that now seemed to be expanding and rippling in his head. There was a host of strange bright things flitting there, but none of them had quite this fierce gay voice. It must be someone he had known only slightly, if at all. "You sound as if you might be a luminary," he said doubtfully.

The voice pounced on this, warmly. "So you *do* remember! Thank goodness for that! Look at me. It may help."

Still puzzled, Sirius frowned in the direction of the voice, along the band of sunlight where he lay, into the blazing white and yellow heart of the sun itself. Under his eyes, the searing light shifted. It flowed and hardened and became a figure, which seemed to be made of the light itself. In shape, it was not unlike a human. But it had fierce white-yellow rays lifting and falling about it and massed around its head like a mane of hair. The queerest thing about it was that Sirius could not tell whether it was a tiny figure quite near, or a large figure very far away. It could have been standing somewhere near the top of the yard wall, or in the very heart of the sun.

"Effulgency," said Sirius, "I'm very sorry. I've been very stupid. You're the Denizen of our luminary, aren't you?"

"That's right," said the bright figure. "The Sun. Sol, they call me."

He stood blazing cheerfully down on Sirius, so bright and confident in his power that Sirius's heart ached to see him. He knew he had once been like this. Now he was only a creature in this luminary's sphere. That put him in mind of his duty. He stood up, with the rope trailing from his neck, and bowed as a creature should to Sol, lowering his front legs till his fringed forearms lay along the ground.

Sol seemed embarrassed. He put out a hand, shimmering awkwardly. "There's no need to bow, Effulgency. I'm only a minor effulgent. The reason I recognized you was that I used to come under your sphere of office."

"I know." Sirius rose from his bow and sat on his haunches. Now he knew it was Sol, and where he must be, he was embarrassed, too, as far as his misty memories would let him be. Sol's sphere had been his nearest neighbor. He should have known him better. But he did remember that Sol had had rather a name for fierce independence and had highly resented any interference in his sphere. "This is Earth, where I am, isn't it?" he said. "I remember I used to admire it because it was so green. I'm sorry I didn't recognize you. To tell you the truth, I— Well, I don't seem to think like a luminary any more."

Sol appraised him, suffusing him with warmth. "That body they put you in isn't more than half-grown yet. You'll have to wait till it's older before you can remember properly. But I'm glad you know who you are now. I need your help, and I hope I can help you."

Sirius gazed up at him dubiously. "Don't get into trouble. I can't do anything to help you. And if you help me, you may find the high effulgents objecting."

"To blazes with that!" Sol was furious. Rays of anger, intense and white, stood out all around him. The dog part of Sirius trembled to see him. He wondered if he had been that terrifying, ever, when he was angry. "I'll help whom I please in my own sphere!" said Sol. "You may have had the devil's own temper, but I respected you. You let me manage things my own way. And then they go and thrust you here on Earth without a word to me! No warning, no instructions. Not even a polite hint. The first I knew of this ridiculous sentence was a wretched little star out of Ursa Minor coming along to tell me we were all under Polaris now. *Polaris!*" He flamed with disgust.

"Polaris?" There was an uncomfortable boiling in Sirius's great green memories. Out of it came a mild, clear-sighted Cepheid, a tall-stander whom he thought he had once liked.

"Yes. Polaris," said Sol, with the mane of rage lifting and falling around him. "One of your Judges, I understand. He may be all right, but he's a Cepheid. And what does a four-day Cepheid understand about my system here? Nothing! And to crown it all, the replacement in your sphere is some blasted amateur from the Castor complex—"

"Castor?" said Sirius. He felt a huge uneasiness, which made the hair stand up all down his back. He could not remember what he knew about the Castor people—except that they were vague and untrustworthy, and too many for their sphere, so that they were always trying to meddle with other people's. "Tell me, Sol— Do you know—? My Companion— Is she—?"

"Still in her sphere, as far as I know," said Sol. He was anxious to get on with his grievance. "It's just as well they didn't trust that amateur on his own. He's set up some kind of trepidation that's almost knocked my outer planet off course, and the next thing I knew there were floods, droughts and famines all over Earth, too. Now I may not be a high effulgent, but there are creatures here, and they're my responsibility. I can't have another Ice Age on Earth yet. So I went and gave Polaris a piece of my mind."

Sirius could not help laughing. He could just see Sol doing it. "Did you?"

"Yes," said Sol. "And I don't think Polaris was very pleased. I told him just what I thought of this New-Sirius of his, and what he's done to Pluto, and to Earth. And he turns round, cool as a cinder, and tells me that there's nothing he can do, because the Sirius Zoi is missing and it's loose in my system somewhere. A Z-z-z-zoi!" Sol said, angrily imitating Polaris.

Sirius jumped up and ran the full length of his rope toward Sol, nearly choking himself in his excitement. "What is this Zoi? Where is it?"

"Don't you know?" said Sol. The rays of rage floated back against him and he became silvery somber with disappointment. "I was hoping you'd remember. I've never seen a Zoi. We don't need power like that here. It's far too strong for us. You *must* know what it's like. You must have used this one."

"Yes, but I can't remember," Sirius said desperately. "I know I've got to find it, but I don't know what it is or what it looks like. I don't even know why I'm here like this. Don't *you* know?"

Sol laughed, a fierce little spurt of fire. "Then we're both in the dark—hardly the right place for luminaries, is it? All I was told is that you're looking for the Zoi. I didn't go to your trial—I've too much to do here—but I *was* told that you lost your temper once too often and somebody's sphere went nova over it. Does that bring anything back to you?"

Sirius sank down and put his head on his paws. "No," he said miserably. "Not a thing. And have you no idea where this Zoi is?"

"It fell on Earth," Sol said, frowning a little. "I'm sure of that now. A lot of things fall here, because there's a belt of asteroids, and things come in from it all the time. But one came in with an almighty bump about six months ago. I didn't pay much attention to it at the time, but I think it may have been the Zoi."

"So they put me on the right world?" Sirius said. It was good to know that, even if it was a little puzzling—almost as if somebody knew.

Sol seemed puzzled as well. He continued to frown, shot with red and orange as he thought. "Look here," he said, "I'm beginning to think there's been some jiggery-pokery somewhere. Your sentence was odd enough. Then they put you in the right place and don't tell me— That makes me so angry that if that Zoi wasn't messing up my whole system I'd leave them to it! Then there's you— Did you kill that luminary, or don't you know?"

Sirius lay and searched among welling, wheeling green things. He found strange facts there, and stranger faces, and terrible sadness. He found rage in plenty. But nowhere, as far as he knew, could he see anything approaching the kind of violence Sol meant. There was nothing even approaching the things he had seen on the television. "No," he said. "I don't think so."

"I wouldn't have thought so, myself," Sol said cheerfully, "from what I know of you. When you got angry, there was usually a good reason for it. So it looks as if someone may be out to injure you. And, since they've so kindly made you one of my creatures, they'll have me to reckon with now. I'm not going to stand for this kind of thing. Would you mind if I made a few inquiries about that trial of yours?"

"Not at all," said Sirius. He could see there would be no stopping Sol anyway. He was so heartened to have a being like Sol on his side that he grinned, a dog's grin, with his tongue out and his head up. "Thank you."

"And I'd like you to get out and look for that Zoi," said Sol. "I think you'd know it if you saw it—which is more than I would. But—are you tied up all the time?"

"I can slip my collar," said Sirius, "but I can't open that gate." His grin faded, and all the boredom and frustration of being shut in the yard came back to him. "Sol—" He looked up at the burning near-and-far figure imploringly. "Please, Effulgency, can't you help me open that gate?"

Sol was both touched and embarrassed that the one-time Denizen of Sirius should appeal to him like this. The plumes of light lifted and shifted around his head, and rays fell crisscross over the gate as Sol made a great play of examining it in order to cover up his feelings. "The bolts and the latch are horribly rusty," he said. "Oxidization of iron, you know, due to the presence of water—"

Sirius was amused. "Teach your grandmother, Sol. Can you or can't you?"

Sol beamed at him, still rather flustered. "Well, you won't be able to reach the top bolt until you've grown a bit. You'll have to wait until after my winter solstice before you'll be big enough. But I can settle the rust for you, so that you'll be able to draw the bolts when you can reach them."

This was immensely heartening. Sirius felt he could wait years, so long as he knew he would get out of the yard in the end. He grinned his wide dog's grin and tried to set Sol at ease with a joke. "So you'll help me to help myself. Is that how things work in your system?"

"Of course." Sol was rather indignant. "Why? Is it different anywhere else?"

"I was trying to make a joke," Sirius explained hastily. "I'm very grateful to you. Please don't be embarrassed any more."

Sol stood in his bar of light and flared with laughter. "You're quite right. I did feel a bit awkward having you for a creature in my sphere. But you're not half as awesome as I expected."

"Awesome?" said Sirius, bristling suspiciously.

"That was a joke too," said Sol. "Almost. I shall have to go now. I've no end of things to do."

"Come and talk to me again," Sirius called as Sol turned away.

"Of course," said Sol. He beamed at Sirius over his shoulder and walked swiftly away up his bar of light, receding and dwindling as he went. Sirius, watching, was reminded of the way the picture in the television dwindled to a silver lozenge when someone turned it off. For a moment, he felt quite strange to be getting a creature's view of a luminary. Then he remembered he was a creature. But it did not bother him as much as it would have done an hour ago. Sol had left behind him a wave of warmth and well-being and joy, and Sirius rolled over and stretched in it, just as the cats did in front of a fire.

6 SIRIUS FOUND lying in the yard easier to endure after this. He knew he would get out in the end. Sol had said so. And if he felt too bored and miserable, he would stretch himself out in the bar of sunlight, knowing Sol would be aware of him. Most of the time, Sol was too busy for more than a hasty greeting before he swept on his way, but this Sirius quite understood. He remembered being busy himself once. And he was very grateful to Sol. Sirius did not know whether it was simply talking to another luminary, or some power in Sol himself, but those vast green thoughts now seemed like a proper part of him and did not keep escaping out of sight as they did before. He still could not see them all. But they were with him, and Sol had done it.

As Sirius watched Sol going about his business, he was

inclined to think it was a special power in Sol. He was amazed at the amount Sol did. Sirius himself had done a great deal. But then his sphere had been incomparably bigger, and he knew that, whatever the Zoi was, he had used it to help him. Sol was a young and joyous luminary, but he did more than Sirius could believe possible, and he did it without a Zoi. Sirius began to suspect that Sol had more life and power in one lifting plume than many luminaries had in their entire sphere.

"I think you were right to say you didn't need a Zoi," he told Sol one evening, as he sank toward the roofs opposite. "You're rather an exceptional luminary, aren't you?"

Sol blazed red and gold laughter into his eyes. "So-so."

Basil happened to be in the yard just then. "That Rat of yours must have the most peculiar eyes," he told Kathleen. "I saw him looking straight at the sun a minute ago, and he didn't even blink."

"I told you—he's very exceptional," said Kathleen.

Proud as she was of her Leo, Kathleen could not help wishing he would not grow so horribly fast. It was quite natural. Sirius was growing into a big dog and he had not much more than a year to do it in. But Kathleen had moments of panic. The smart red collar was soon far too small and she had to buy another. Sirius, to his annoyance, had to go through the whole business of secretly scratching a raw spot until Kathleen made the new collar loose enough to slip off. And then he had it all to do again just after Christmas, when he found he had grown again. Kathleen never dared tell Duffie just how much Leo ate, and he always seemed rather too thin. She took a book on dog care out of the library and worried about him.

"What's the matter?" said Mr. Duffield, a little before Christmas, finding Kathleen staring wanly at an open book.

"It's Leo, Uncle Harry," said Kathleen. "I'm not feeding him right."

Mr. Duffield looked down at Sirius, and Sirius thumped his heavy tail in acknowledgment. Sirius's feathery coat was a glossy cream color, his nose was black and wet and his eyes were green and bright. His legs, with their fringes of curly hair, were awkwardly long and would not fold under him, but they were straight and strong. He had a surprisingly narrow waist, but Mr. Duffield could only see two of his ribs beyond it. "He looks all right to me," Mr. Duffield said. "Growing into rather an elegant creature, isn't he? What's wrong?"

"He weighs as much as Robin," Kathleen explained. "We balanced them on a plank in the yard yesterday. And it says here that dogs who weigh that much ought to have a *pound* of raw meat every day!"

"Good grief!" said Mr. Duffield. "I weigh three times more than that. We're both being underfed. Would fifty pence a week help you support your horse?"

"Oh *thank* you!" said Kathleen. She had not the heart to explain that meat cost a great deal more than that. And fifty pence did help. By scrimping and saving, making Christmas presents for everyone herself and being very sweet and cajoling to the butcher, Kathleen managed to buy Leo raw lights every other day, and still saved enough to give him a red rubber ball for Christmas.

Sirius enjoyed the ball hugely. But Christmas was not a happy time. Nobody except Mr. Duffield bothered to give Kathleen anything. He gave her a book-token, which Duffie said was a waste of money, since Kathleen had a dog, didn't she? And Kathleen had never cooked a turkey before. In her anxiety, she overcooked it and it was dry. Sirius and the cats ate dry turkey until they nearly burst. Duffie expressed herself savagely.

"If you want your turkey properly cooked," said Mr. Duffield, "you might consider cooking it yourself." As soon as the shops opened again, he took Kathleen out and bought her a new dress. Kathleen was delighted. The dress was a bright blue which matched her eyes. Sirius thought she looked enchanting in it. He tried to tell her so by bounding and squeaking, and he was so grateful to Mr. Duffield that he put his great front paws on his knee and licked his face. "Go away!" said Mr. Duffield, pushing him off. "I know she looks nice, but there's no call to wash me for it." He said to Kathleen, "You'd almost think that creature understands what goes on."

"Oh, he does," Kathleen said earnestly. "He knows English." Sirius was surprised to hear her say that. He had not thought she had noticed. But Mr. Duffield just thought it was the expression of a touching faith in Kathleen, and he laughed at her.

Early in the New Year, an oil truck scraped and groaned its way along the back of the houses, through the lane behind the Duffields' yard. The neighbors, two houses on, had installed central heating, and their fuel tank was awkwardly placed. Sirius sat up in the yard, a high and narrow dog these days, watching the men leaning out and cursing and the lorry grinding backwards and forwards, and wondered what was going on. He soon saw. As the truck came level with the yard gate for the third time, the heavy gray clouds that covered the sky parted for a moment, letting through a silvery shaft of light. The lorry gleamed. Then, somehow, oil was spurting from it, spraying the gate all over, until it was black and dripping. Sirius threw back his head and laughed his dog's laugh toward the place where the clouds had parted.

"Thank you!"

Then the smell rolled over his sensitive nose. He backed away, sneezing and choking and frantically pawing his face. The men in the tanker, equally frantic, ran about shouting and turning stopcocks. Duffie stormed out from the house and spoke cold and shrill about careless idiots and the risk of fire.

Sirius rather thought Duffie got some money from the oil company to replace the gate. But nobody touched the gate. The Duffield family seldom bothered with things like that and, besides, the weather turned terrible. For six weeks, rain lashed down, hail bounced in the yard, and it grew colder daily. Sirius lay shivering in his shelter, watching sleet pile into transparent drifts with bubbles embalmed in them, and then the rain rattle down and melt the drifts again. He spoke to Sol about it, rather reproachfully, in one of the few glimpses he had of him.

"Blame the Zoi for some of it," said Sol. "But you creatures always grumble about precipitation. You'd grumble even worse if you didn't get it. It won't hurt you to wait a month. And you didn't want to live with that smell of oil, did you?"

"No," said Sirius. "That's true. Thanks."

At the end of February, the weather turned mild and chilly. By this time, the gate was clean, except for the fastenings, which were black and sticky still. Sol beamed pale yellow from a pale blue sky. "You're not far off full grown now," he observed. "How's your memory?"

"Not very good," Sirius said glumly. Though his green nature was now always with him, his dog nature lay warm and stupid in front of it, just behind his eyes, and blotted out great tracts of the green.

"It's bound to improve," Sol said cheerfully, and strode on his way.

Sirius stood up and stretched, almost as carefully and thoroughly as Tibbles did. Tibbles herself was sitting on the wall. She watched, rather offended. When Sirius finished, she sneezed and was about to turn away. But her lime-green eyes widened and she stared when Sirius, instead of lying down again, backed firmly to the end of his rope and went on backing. His collar slid up over his ears, stuck a moment and then fell off over his nose.

"That was clever," Tibbles said. "Can you get it back on again?"

"I expect so," said Sirius. He advanced on the gate, waving his tail joyfully. "Can you show me how to get this open?"

"We are bold, aren't we?" said Tibbles. "I've told you— I can do the bolt at the bottom, but I can't reach the other fastenings."

"I can reach the others if you show me how they work," said Sirius.

"Very well." Rather humped and grudging, Tibbles descended from the wall and sat elegantly down at the base of the gate. Sirius watched carefully as she extended a narrow white paw to the knob of the bolt, delicately pushed the knob upward and then patted it gently until it slid greasily back in the oily slot. "There. Can you do that?" she said, sure that he could not.

"I don't know. I'll try." Sirius raised himself on his hind legs and leaned against the gate, full stretch. Like that, he was now rather taller than Kathleen. The top bolt was within easy reach of his clumsy right paw. He raised the paw and batted at the bolt with it. Luckily, it was slightly stiffer. The knob went up to the right position and stuck there, and Sirius had to come down for a rest at that stage. Tibbles looked superior. But Sirius heaved himself up on his back legs again and gave the knob a sideways swipe, hasty and strong. As he sank down, the bolt went rattling back.

"That was quite clever," Tibbles said patronizingly.

"That's what I thought," said Sirius. "How does the latch undo?"

"You push it up—that little sharp bit that sticks out," Tibbles said.

Sirius tried. The gate jumped about in its moorings, but nothing else happened.

"Stupid," said Tibbles. "Here, let me stand on your back and I'll show you."

"All right." Sirius stood with his side against the gate, and Tibbles leaped easily up to the middle of his back. Both of them hated it. Sirius's hackles went up, and he only just prevented himself snapping at Tibbles. And Tibbles felt so insecure that she dug all her claws into him, hard. Sirius rumbled out a growl, which made Tibbles's hair stand up too.

"Listen," she snapped. "I'm doing you a kindness."

"I know!" Sirius snarled, craning around to see what she was up to. "Be quick."

Tibbles put out a shaky paw and lifted the latch. Sirius had barely time to understand he had been hitting the wrong part, before Tibbles jumped clear. They stood glaring at one another, while, behind Sirius, the gate swung creaking open into the lane.

"Thank you," said Sirius.

"You're welcome." Tibbles's fur was still up. She raised one paw and gave it a quick, irritated licking. "That's the last time I stand on a dog."

"That's the last time I let you." Sirius bent his tall narrow body into a half-circle and looked out into the lane. It was empty. He slid through the gap, and then threw himself joyfully backwards at the gate. It shut, with a slam and a click. He was free. He put his nose down and was about to scour away down the lane.

"I say!" Tibbles was on the wall, crouching to look down at him.

"What?" he said impatiently.

"When you come back," Tibbles said, "you'll find that side's easier to open. You have to tread on the flat bit, then go away backwards so that the gate can open. Do you understand?"

"Yes, yes. I think so." Sirius did not like to tell her that he had no intention of coming back. He galloped off down the lane, flinging a glad good-by over his shoulder to Tibbles, and began the most marvelous day of his life.

His dog nature needed a free rein first. It cried out to examine every whiff and stink he passed, to raise its leg at every lamppost and corner, and to run up the pavement as it had seldom run before. When the joy of that subsided a little, Sirius remembered he had an errand. He turned and crossed the road.

Kathleen had tried to teach him about cars. Sirius did look to see that there was a gap to cross in. But only experience teaches you how fast a car can move. Hooters and brakes screamed. Sirius tore out from beneath the skidding wheels of one motorist, only to find another rushing at him from the other side. The second motorist only missed him because a sudden blaze of sunlight startled him into jerking his wheel to the right. Sirius, shaken to his green core, bolted into an alleyway opposite and lay down panting in its shadow.

"That was stupid of you," Sol said, gilding the wall in front of him. "I'll leave you to be squashed if you do that again."

"Sorry," panted Sirius.

"I should hope so!" said Sol. "Now listen. I've been checking up on the things that fell here last spring, and there are six that could be the Zoi. Four of them went down in Great Britain, and the other two in France. It does look more and more as if someone knew where to put you. It worries me. Start looking, won't you?"

"I am looking," said Sirius. He arose with great dignity and trotted purposefully off.

He honestly intended to search. But he had not realized until that day how big and how full of interest was the town where he lived. He kept having adventures. He met children in parks, cats on fences and women in shops. And outside the Town Hall he met two policemen.

The policemen sprang suddenly out of a car parked in front of the Town Hall and advanced purposefully on Sirius, one from either side.

"Here, doggie. Come here. Nice fellow," said one.

Sirius looked up and saw at once they were trying to catch him. It must be because he had no collar. Behind them, traffic was thundering along the road. Sirius dared not dash across it after what Sol had said. He wondered whether to dash the other way, up the steps of the Town Hall, but a party of people were coming down them—people in dark clothes, with the smell of importance clinging to them. Unless he was very clever, he was going to be caught.

"Nice fellow," said the policeman behind him. "Here!"

Sirius turned to him, his tail waving, his ears down, and his mouth open jovially. When he had put himself in a position from which he could see both policemen, he stopped and bent his elbows to the pavement, wagged his tail furiously and gave an encouraging bark.

"Thinks we're playing," said the first policeman.

Both policemen grabbed. Sirius dodged. They grabbed again, and he bounced away between them, barking delightedly. They moved far more slowly than Robin or Basil. Another bounce or so, and he would be able to make off down the nearest side street.

"What is it, Constable? A stray?" called the Lord Mayor from the steps. He was a dog-lover. "Can we help?"

"Well, if you could catch hold of him, sir—" said the first policeman. Both of them were sweating by now.

Most willingly, the Lord Mayor came down the steps. With him came the Town Clerk, the Borough Surveyor, three Councilors, and the Lord Mayor's chauffeur. Sirius suddenly found himself having to dodge a whole crowd of people. He dodged and he bounced and he barked, and he led them in a mad dance down the pavement. They got in one another's way. Sirius was able to dash off down a side road, barking excitedly, looking as if he thought this was the greatest game of his life. In a way it was. He was laughing widely as he collapsed to rest behind a row of dustbins. He had never had such fun.

The dustbins smelled most fetchingly. All this running had made Sirius ravenous. He got up and tracked the fetching smell to the third dustbin along. It was a measure of how much he had learned that interesting morning, that he had no difficulty at all in prizing the lid off it. Inside, wrapped in newspaper, were the remains of a fried chicken. Sirius took it out and nosed aside the paper. The chicken was already in his mouth, when an old lady, attracted by the clang of the lid on the roadway, came hobbling down the steps of her house.

"Leave!" she said sternly.

Sirius looked up at her, hardly able to credit it.

"Drop it!" she commanded. "You heard me." When Sirius did nothing but stare, the old lady seized the chicken and wrenched it from his mouth. Sirius growled and tried to hang on. "No you don't!" said the intrepid old lady. She was so fierce that Sirius stopped growling and watched hopelessly while the old lady put the chicken back in the dustbin and rammed the lid on. He could not help whining a little at that. "Oh no," said the old lady. "Not chicken bones, and not out of dustbins. I'm not going to stand by and see a nice dog like you ruin his insides. Don't you know chicken bones splinter? You'd die in agony, dog. Come with me and I'll find you something else."

She turned and began to hobble back up her steps. Sirius

climbed up behind her, rather interested. Indoors, she limped to a tiny kitchen and opened a very small refrigerator.

"Let's see," she said. "Not a pork chop, I think. But here's a bit of stewing beef you can have. Here." She handed over a succulent lump. It vanished at once. "I can't think why you dogs never wait to taste anything," the old lady said. "Would you like some cake? It's bad for teeth, but it's better than chicken." Sirius pranced beside her eagerly to a small cupboard. He was given nearly half a big currant cake. "Better now?" asked the old lady.

Sirius showed her he was by wagging his tail and nosing her twisted old hand. The twisted old hand turned and stroked his ears like an expert. Even Kathleen did not stroke ears so well. "You're a beauty," said the old lady. "I lost my dog a year ago. I'd love to keep you, but I can see you're well cared for. Slipped your collar, naughty dog. I bet you belong to some little girl who'd break her heart if she lost you. Yes. Surprised you, didn't I?" she said, as Sirius stared at her. "I know dogs. My Lass used to understand English too. Now, I'm going to let you out and you're to go *home*. Understand?"

Sirius understood perfectly. He felt extremely guilty as he set off trotting in quite the opposite direction. But he had to be free to find that Zoi.

He came to an area of little houses in a tight crisscross of small streets near the river. The river was dark and slimy. Sirius did not care for it. He went swiftly away from it, up the nearest street, and heard paws excitedly bang on a wooden gate he was passing. Some dog whined:

"Hey! I say! Hallo, hallo, hallo!"

Sirius stopped. It was a gate to a yard a little smaller than his own, and nothing like such a high one. There was wire netting nailed across the bottom of the gate, and more wire netting above it and above the fence beyond, making this yard even more of a prison than his own. Feeling very sympathetic, Sirius lay down and looked through the lower netting. The other dog lay down at the same moment. They stared at one another, nose to nose. Sirius's tail arched in astonishment. It was almost like looking in a mirror. This was a bitch, and she had soft brown eyes, but she had the same creamy, feathery coat, and the same red ears. She was very handsome.

"Who are you?" said Sirius. "Why do you look like me?"

"Who are you? I'm Patchie. Hallo, hallo, hallo," said the other dog.

"Hallo," he said. "They call me Leo."

"Hallo, Leo. Hallo, hallo!" said she.

"Don't you say anything else but Hallo?"

"What else is there to say? Hallo, hallo."

"There are all sorts of other things to say. Do you find it very boring, shut up in that yard?"

"Why should I?" she said, in some surprise. "Hallo."

"Oh well," said Sirius. "You don't happen to know what a Zoi is, do you?"

"No," she said. "A bone? Hallo. Who's your master?"

"I haven't got a master. A girl called Kathleen takes care of me."

"Poor you!" said Patchie. "My master's called Ken. He's *lovely!*"

It suddenly dawned on Sirius that this was the most stupid creature he had ever encountered. He hoisted himself to his feet, bitterly disappointed. "I must go."

"Come back tomorrow. Good-by, good-by, good-by!" said Patchie.

No fear! thought Sirius, and trotted off.

Two gates farther on, there was another creamy dog with red ears. He leaped and whined and hurled himself at his netting. "Hallo, hallo! I saw you go down and I hoped you'd come back. Hallo, hallo. I'm Bruce. Hallo."

"Hallo," Sirius said politely, and passed on.

Farther up the street, there were two more cream and red dogs, Rover and Redears, and they, too, were uncannily like Sirius. Sirius was bewildered. No other dogs he had met looked like this. "Why do you look like me?" he asked Redears.

"Oh hallo, hallo, hallo!" Redears answered. "Because we're both dogs, I suppose. Hallo."

"Don't any of you ever say anything but Hallo?" Sirius said, quite exasperated.

"Of course not. That's what dogs say," said Redears. "Hallo."

Sirius wanted to tell him to go and get lost in a tin of cat food, but he supposed Redears could not help being stupid. He said good-by politely and went on. Now I know what Basil means when he calls people morons, he thought. What idiots!

A little farther on, the crisscross streets were being knocked down. Sirius spent some time watching bulldozers plow heaps of bricks about. Some men in yellow helmets made a fuss of him and gave him a ham sandwich. They seemed to think he was one of the four moronic hallo-dogs.

"Here! Isn't this your Bruce got out again?" one of them shouted to the man in the bulldozer.

"No," bellowed the man. "Must be Rover or Redears. Can't tell them apart."

While they were bawling to one another, Sirius slipped off and came to a wide cindery place where all the houses had been cleared away. It ended in a part which had evidently been knocked down, but not cleared, some years before. There were big heaps of rubble, with bare bushes and small trees sprouting from them. The bricks and cinders were covered with white grass and the dry stalks of tall weeds.

As Sirius pushed his way through, he felt a tingle. It was more than a smell, bigger than a feeling. It was tingling, living, huge. He froze, with his head up. Only a Zoi could feel like that. It *must* be the Zoi. But the tingle was gone as he froze. Sirius strained nose, ears, everything, to catch it again. But there was nothing. Perhaps the wind had changed. Sirius ran to and fro, casting for the scent, or feeling, or whatever it was, almost frantic. There was nothing, absolutely nothing. He seemed to have lost the Zoi the moment he found it. Despairingly, he looked up at Sol.

Sol was much lower down the sky than he expected. Another anxiety came over Sirius. "What time is it?"

"Half past three Greenwich," said Sol. "What's the matter?"

For a moment, Sirius felt he was being torn in two. The Zoi was here somewhere. He knew it was. But Kathleen would be home from school just after four. He had barely time to get back. He turned and set off trotting fast in what his dog sense told him was the way home. "The Zoi," he said over his shoulder to Sol. "It's somewhere quite near. But I can't stay." He was angry with himself. The dog in him had cheated his green nature by lying cunningly low until the last moment. It had intended to go home all the time. "I can't *help* it!" he told Sol angrily.

"Of course not," said Sol. "You can come here tomorrow. I'll try and trace the thing which fell nearest here."

7

LIKE THE WIND, and straight as a die, Sirius made for home. He passed a number of people on the way who tried to stop him and talk to him. "Here, boy. Nice dog." But Sirius was in too much of a hurry to attend. He went straight past their inviting hands without pausing or turning aside. He crossed roads, quickly but carefully. By the time he reached the lane behind the yard, Sol was behind the houses, at least another half hour down, and Sirius was almost too tired and puffed to trot.

"There you are at last!" said Tibbles.

Sirius looked up to see her, and Romulus and Remus, sitting in an anxious huddle on the wall by the gate. He was astonished—and touched and pleased—to see they had all been worrying about him. Then he was alarmed. "Has Duffie noticed I was gone?"

"Not *she*," said Remus.

"Kathleen's coming down the street in front," said Romulus.

Sirius did not have time to think how to undo the latch. He simply upped and trod on it, and sprang away backwards, hoping. The gate swung open. Sirius stumbled wearily inside.

"Shut it," said Tibbles. "Unless you want that collar tightened."

Groaning, Sirius faced the gate and wondered how he could shut it. The latch was within reach of his mouth. He could only try. He put his teeth around the unpleasant oily rusty-tasting metal and dragged backwards. The gate swung, and clicked shut. "Thank goodness for that!" Sirius made for his collar, lying at the end of its rope. If he had had time to think how to get it on, he would probably not have been able to do it. But he was in such a panic that his green intelligence swept aside his dog stupidity. Without thinking, he lay down, propped the empty collar between both front paws, put his head into it and pushed. Then he keeled over on his side, wanting only to sleep, and rather thinking he might die.

But there was no time to sleep, or to die either. Kathleen was there the next minute, undoing the rope. "There, Leo. I hope you weren't too lonely. Walk!"

He was forced to stagger off to the meadow for a walk. His paws hurt, his legs ached, his back ached. He became convinced he was dying. He waded miserably into the river, and, when that failed to soothe his aches, he sat on the bank with his head hanging and eight inches or so of purplish tongue dangling from his jaws.

"Oh dear!" said Kathleen. "Leo, I don't think you're well."

She brought him home. He fell on the hearthrug with a thump and went straight to sleep.

"Robin, something's wrong with Leo," said Kathleen. "I thing he's ill."

"Distemper, perhaps?" said Robin. He and Basil rolled Sirius about, shouting, "Wake up, Shamus! *Rat!*" They woke Sirius up. He groaned piteously, to show them he needed to be left in peace to die, and fell asleep again. "Leave him," said Basil. "He may sleep it off."

Sirius slept until Kathleen's bedtime, and only a strong sense of duty roused him then. He staggered to the kitchen, where he ate and drank hugely. Then he limped upstairs after Kathleen, wanting only to go to sleep again. Kathleen saw that playing games was out of the question. She read him the story of Bluebeard instead. Sirius could hardly keep his eyes open.

"Silly fool!" said Tibbles, stepping delicately in through the window.

"Yes. I'll know another time," said Sirius. Then he fell asleep and, to Tibbles's disgust, he snored and twitched. He dreamed he was out in the street again, running with four dogs just like himself.

To Kathleen's relief, Leo was quite restored in the morning. He bounded willingly out into the yard and did not seem to mind being tied up at all. "You *are* a good dog," she said, and she hugged him uncomfortably before she left. As soon as she was well away, Sirius sprang up and slipped his collar off. He found that Tibbles had prudently bolted the bottom bolt on the gate again, but that was no trouble now. It went back with one swipe of his paw. He used his nose to lift the latch. Now he knew the Zoi was somewhere near, he told himself he would take things more steadily and search until he had found it.

As he was shutting the gate, Sol stepped up above the house. "You must be right," he said. He seemed irritable. Fierce little spurts of light shot from him. "Something did fall in this area somewhere. But it's very odd. I just can't see it—and I can see every stone and every blade of grass."

"Could it have gone into the ground?" asked Sirius.

"It must have done," said Sol. "So I can't think why Earth hasn't noticed it. It came down with a big enough thump. Yet there's no damage. Is a Zoi something very small and dense?"

Sirius sat down and tried to marshal vague green memories. What *was* a Zoi like? The trouble was, it was something he had used every day for long ages, and it had become so familiar that he had barely noticed it. "I don't think it was always the same," he said doubtfully. "I—I can't describe it."

Sol spurted spiky annoyance. "You're worse than the rest of them! Think, can't you!"

"I can't," said Sirius. The warm dog thoughts sat just behind his eyes again, and he felt miserably stupid. "But I'd know it when I saw it."

"Don't droop like that," said Sol. "I'm sorry. It's not your fault I was sharp. I've been having a rather annoying time trying to find out about Zoi. Everyone tells me something different. The only thing they agree on is that I seem to have had a narrow escape. The thing must have gone right past me. They say I was lucky not to have my sphere go nova."

"Oh, no," Sirius said, out of his green memories, without having to think. "Whoever told you that didn't know much about Zoi. They can't act unless someone has hold of them."

"Ah," said Sol. His spurting plumes floated thoughtfully down around him. "Then the rumor that you flung this Zoi at that luminary is out, isn't it? Do you think you can get on and find it before the wrong kind of person lays hold of it? I've no wish to have my sphere go nova."

Sirius wondered who Sol had been talking to. He found himself bristling with queer suspicions. "What are you getting at?"

"I've a number of people in mind," said Sol. "Humans and animals aren't the only creatures to get born on Earth, you know. Some of the darker ones are pretty strange and rather formidable. I suggest you go back to where you caught that whiff of the Zoi and start from there."

"All right," said Sirius, still rather puzzled.

He went on his way at a swift trot toward the cleared space, wondering, as he went, what was really in Sol's mind. He had a feeling Sol knew much more than he had said. But that went out of his head when he caught a tingle from the Zoi again. It came from behind him, and it was gone as soon as he felt it. Nevertheless, he set off toward it. He was almost back at the yard, when he caught it again—a swift, living tingle from quite a new direction. He set off that way, but it was gone. On the outskirts of the town, he caught it again, from a new direction. Thoroughly confused, he turned back.

"What are you doing?" Sol wanted to know.

"I've felt it three times—from a different place each time," Sirius explained.

"Could someone be trying to confuse you?" Sol asked.

Sirius tried to consider this. It was not easy, because he was tired now, and the dog stupidity was down on his brain like a low cloud. "It could be the Zoi itself," he said doubtfully. "It—it isn't made of quite the same stuff as anything else. I can't explain properly, but I know it can work in several directions at once."

"I hope it is only that," said Sol. "You'd better go at it systematically. Take one small area and search that. Then go on to the next. I'm sorry to bully you like this, but I think it's urgent."

Again Sirius was puzzled. "A month ago you were saying it wouldn't hurt me to wait," he protested. "What's got into you?"

Sol gave a little flare of laughter. "Call it my fiery and impatient nature. No, seriously, now I've heard a little more about Zoi, I can see they're a good deal more peculiar and powerful than I thought. This one could do a lot of damage, and I want it found."

Sirius trotted back to the center of town. He thought he would sweep the town in a spiral, to see if he could pinpoint the Zoi that way first. But, finding himself near the street where he had tried to rob the dustbin, he suddenly felt ravenous. He climbed the steps of the old lady's house and, in the most natural way, battered at her door with a heavy clawed foot.

"So it's you again," she said, opening it. "I might have known." She put a gnarled hand under his jaw and looked at him. "Naughty dog. Out again. I don't know what your name really is, but I'm going to call you Sirius, because of your eyes. I am Miss Smith. Come in, Sirius, and I'll see what I can find. And I expect you'll want a drink."

It was the start of a long acquaintance. After that, Sirius visited her nearly every day. It was not only because, poor though she evidently was, Miss Smith always had something for him to eat. He liked and respected her too. Apart from Kathleen, she was the only person who saw he understood English, and she called him by his one-time true name. Just as Kathleen did, she talked to him as if he was nearly her equal. And then he realized that she looked forward to seeing him and saved food for him specially. After that, he would no more have missed his daily visit to Miss Smith than he would have failed to be home in the yard before Kathleen was.

His search for the Zoi went on week after week. He felt it over and over again, always just for an instant, but he simply could not pin down where the feeling was coming from. The living tang came now from this way, now from that. Sometimes he did not feel it for days on end. He gave up chasing it when he did feel it. He always arrived at the outskirts of the town, only to feel it behind him, somewhere inside the town. At times, he almost agreed with Sol, that someone was deliberately confusing him. He took Sol's impatient advice and searched the town, section by section. It seemed to him that if he could build up a picture of the town in his head, with all the places plotted on it where he had felt the Zoi, the middle of the plottings must be where the Zoi was.

It was very difficult. For one thing, his green nature became angry and bored. It seemed used to settling things quickly. To his surprise, it was his dog nature that helped him here. It was used to being bored, and it seemed to be able to stick patiently to its work, long after the luminary was howling with impatience. He began to see why humans had the word *dogged*.

But Sirius's great difficulty was that neither of his natures could hold a useful picture of the town in its head. The dog saw it all as fragments, smells and the way to other fragments and smells. The green thoughts would try to bend it all into a sphere. But Sirius wanted a complete picture, flat and whole, the way humans liked to have things. The only one he knew of was in Basil's room. Basil had an actual map of the town pinned to his wall. Whenever he could, Sirius nosed open Basil's door and sat on the mat by Basil's bed, staring at the map and trying to make sense of the symbols Basil had carefully painted on it.

Basil was furious when he found him there. "Get out, Rat! Beat it, or I'll jump on your tail!" The room was full of tiny pieces of rock and bits of old pottery spread on half-made plans and charts. Sirius could have spoiled them all with one sweep of his tail. Basil did not know he had been careful not to. He shut the door and warned Kathleen to keep it shut. Sirius could not open the door for himself. In order to find out more about the map, he began, for the first time since he was a puppy, to attend to what Basil was saying.

Basil had a friend with glasses called Clive. Basil very much admired Clive—Sirius thought Clive was probably cleverer than Basil—and whenever Clive called, Basil became enormously enthusiastic about rocks and old pottery and imitated the way Clive talked. Clive called the bits and pieces Remains. Basil and he collected Remains of all kinds, and made maps of where they had found them. Many of the Remains were called fossils. Sirius thought they looked like playthings of Sol's when he was an infant. He could not see any value in them. He could see even less value in the pottery, which Clive said was Roman, though he supposed some of the old coins they had must have been valuable once.

The pride of their collection were some blue beads they had found in the cleared area near the moronic hallo-dogs —Clive said repeatedly those ought to have been in the museum—and a small fat meteorite.

None of this was much use to Sirius. He had almost given up listening to them, when he discovered that it was Clive's —and therefore Basil's—ambition to find another meteorite.

"We know one fell near here," Basil said earnestly. "Everyone heard it. They discussed it on television."

"Yes, but I don't see how it could land with a festering thump like that and shake all the houses, and then just disappear," said Clive. "Unless it was a very small black hole —like the one they think fell in Russia."

Sirius realized, to his horror, that they were talking about the Zoi. The hair on his back rose. If Basil got hold of the Zoi—well, if he was not killed by it straight away, he could wreck Sol's sphere in seconds, and maybe other neighboring ones into the bargain. He saw why Sol was so worried.

"If it was a black hole, it would have gone right through the earth," Basil objected, looking uneasily at Sirius. The Rat had that habit of staring at him sometimes. "It would have showed."

"Yes," agreed Clive. "I went and talked to the chap at the museum last Saturday, and he was sure it was just a meteorite. He said they tried to locate it, but the impact was too diffused. All the seismographs in the area went mad, and they all gave different readings. And listen to this, Basil— never mind that festering dog."

Basil had grown tired of Sirius staring at him. He was

making snarling noises and threatening to hit him.

"This is important," said Clive.

"I'm going to put the Rat outside the door first," said Basil. He seized Sirius by his collar and dragged him to the yard door. Sirius braced his legs and resisted, but the hold on his collar, as always, defeated him. He was thrust outside and the door slammed after him.

"What did you do that for?" Kathleen said in the kitchen.

"I don't want Rats around me—or festering Irish morons either," said Basil.

Sirius looked anxiously toward where Sol was westering. "Basil and his friend are trying to find the Zoi too. How can I stop them?"

"I don't think you can," said Sol. "I'll do my best to distract them, but boys are the very blazes. They poke and pry and end up finding things long after everyone else has given up looking. The museum people gave up long ago."

"I hope that was all Clive was going to say," Sirius said.

When Kathleen let him in again, he sneaked up to Basil's room, not very hopefully. He thought he ought to find out how much Basil knew about Zoi. And, to his joy, the door came open when he nosed it. Basil had been in too much of a hurry to show Clive his Remains to remember to close it properly. Sirius went over to the bookshelf and examined the books. He knew humans kept most of their knowledge in books—they were generous like that—and what Basil knew would be there somewhere.

After some thought, he selected one with a picture of a rock on the back, and another with what he supposed was meant to be a galaxy. Between them, they seemed to cover the case. He wished he had Tibbles to get them out for him. He had to do what he could himself, stabbing with a clumsy paw, backed up with his nose. The galaxy-book came out easily enough. He trotted with it to Kathleen's room and laid it on the floor by her bed. Then he came back for the rock-book. The books were looser by then. The rock-book came out with half a shelf-full of heavy volumes. Sirius leaped from among them with his tail tucked under him and trotted away very hastily and guiltily indeed.

"Who's been spilling my books about?" Basil demanded. "Was it you, Robin? If it was—!"

Being accused, Robin naturally looked guilty. "I never went near your books!" Basil cuffed his ears, and Sirius felt very uncomfortable. The worst of it was that there was no possible way he could have owned up, even if he had wanted to.

When Kathleen went to bed, she was very surprised to see the two books lying on the floor. "Those are Basil's! How did they get here?" She picked them up and examined them for clues. Sirius did his best to seem casual. He had carried them as carefully as he knew how and—he hoped—had not left the faintest dent of a toothmark anywhere on them.

Kathleen could not find anything to tell her how the books came to be on her floor. "Oh well," she said. "We may as well read them before we put them back."

Sirius grinned widely as he scrambled onto the bed and made himself comfortable. He had known he could trust Kathleen to read the books. She had few books of her own, and a passion for reading. Once, she had even read him a book of Duffie's on how to make pottery.

She began on the rock-book, because it was on top. *"Schist and gneiss,"* Kathleen read, *"are igneous formations of the Pre-Cambrian era.* Oh, Leo, I don't think this is very interesting. *Metamorphic rocks of high mineral content are to be found as follows*—Leo, I don't know how to say half of this. Shall we try the other book instead?"

She picked up the galaxy-book. It was written in slightly easier words and soon had both of them fascinated. Kathleen was awed and amazed at the thought of stars and planets wheeling around through infinite space. Sirius was amazed at how much humans had discovered, sitting on Earth and whizzing around once every day. They had contrived to measure this, record that and calculate what they could not see. They had a picture of the universe which bore about as much relation to the universe Sirius knew as a Police Identikit picture did to a real person. But he was astonished they had a picture at all.

"It's about luminaries," he explained to Tibbles, when she came through the window to join them. "Do you know about them?"

"The bright people who come and talk to our Sun sometimes?" she said. "They're a bit big to notice me. I'd have to be as big as Earth before I could get to know them. And I don't understand the language anyway. Does the Earth count as one of them?"

"Earth is a planet," Sirius told her. "It spins round the sun."

"That accounts for it," Tibbles said, humping up into a tuffet under Sirius's nose. "The top of my back itches. Just along my spine."

"Accounts for what?" Sirius asked, licking obligingly.

"The way Earth speaks our languages," said Tibbles. "I knew that it must be different."

"Do listen to this, Leo!" Kathleen cried out. "It's about the Dog Star. *Sirius, Alpha Canis Major, often called the Dog Star, is only some eight and a half light-years distant from our Solar System. Since it is twice as hot as our sun, its brightness and characteristic green color make it a notable object in our winter sky.* Why didn't I know that before? I should have called you Sirius, Leo. It's exactly right for you. I *wish* I'd known! You're in Canis Major—that's the Great Dog—and that's Orion's dog, Leo. I *knew* about Orion, too! My Daddy showed me Orion's belt once, when I was little. You're in the same stardrift as the Great Bear—and us, I think, though it doesn't say very clearly—and you're a lovely bright green. Oh—and you've got a Companion that's a white dwarf, about half the size of our sun. Tibbles, you must be his Companion."

Sirius could not avoid sighing heavily. Someone from Castor had his green sphere now, and his Companion too.

"Don't be sad," said Kathleen. "I was just joking. It's far too late to change your name now. You're still Leo."

She went on to read of the other stars. Sirius sighed once or twice more, as he recognized friends of his from the book's descriptions: Betelgeuse, Procon, Canopus and Aldebaran, Rigel, Dubhe, Mizar and Phad. He wondered if he would ever see them again. But he was glad to see, from the way the book talked, that Basil was unlikely to have learned anything helpful about Zoi. The people who wrote the book might be able to measure spheres, and their effulgence, and their distance apart, but they seemed to think they were as lifeless and mechanical as the marbles Robin sometimes rolled around the yard.

8 THOUGH SIRIUS WAS now sure Basil had no idea it was a Zoi he was looking for, he still knew it would be a disaster if Basil found it. As soon as he was out of the yard next day, he went straight to the cleared space where he had first felt the Zoi. It seemed a very likely place for the Zoi to have fallen. But there was nothing. Sirius roved around among the dry weeds and the heaps of rubble without feeling the slightest twinge from the Zoi. So he decided to visit the four moronic hallo-dogs again. They might be stupid, even for dogs, but they fascinated him.

As he went along the street, Rover, Redears and Patchie all greeted him as they had done before.

"Hallo, hallo, hallo! Hey, dog! Hallo!"

But he found he had misjudged Bruce. "Hallo!" Bruce said, hurling himself against the netting around his gate. "I *am* glad to see you again. I wanted to talk to you. The others are such fools, and you look sensible. Why do we all look so alike?"

"I don't know," said Sirius. "I hoped you'd know. Were you all found floating in the river, by any chance?"

"I've no idea," said Bruce. "Is that where dogs come from then?"

"No," Sirius said patiently. "They get born. Didn't you see that mother dog with puppies on television the other night?"

"Oh, yes," said Bruce. "It did make me wonder. Why did you ask about the river then?"

"Because I can remember being picked out of it," said Sirius.

"Good lord! You must have a good memory!" said Bruce. "That must have been months ago."

"But haven't you heard the people you live with talking about where you came from?" Sirius asked.

Bruce confessed that he did not know very much human talk. "I can follow if they speak slowly," he said. "But they will gabble so. All I can usually pick out is the important words like *walk*, and *supper*, and *biscuit*, and *bath*."

"Is *bath* important?" asked Sirius, who had never had one.

Bruce shivered. "Yes. When they say it, they're going to put you in horrible deep warm water and rub smelly bubbles into you that hurt your eyes. They say it when they think you have a flea. Don't your people do that?"

"Certainly not!" said Sirius. "No one in my house would dream of such a thing."

"You are lucky," Bruce said wistfully. "You're lucky to be allowed out too. How do you manage it?"

"I open my gate," said Sirius. "Can't you open yours?"

"Not this latch," said Bruce. "I could open the two they had before this one, so they put this one on to stop me. I'm being rather slow learning it, I'm afraid. But I'll see you outside one day."

"I'll see you," Sirius promised, and he went trotting off, thinking that he rather liked Bruce and feeling pleasantly superior to him—particularly about the baths.

Alas for Sirius. He had now been loose in the town for three weeks. He had talked to innumerable stray dogs and searched for the Zoi in many unsavory places. The next day he began to itch. He itched terribly. He sat down every hundred yards to scratch, but he still itched. He itched when he got home. He sat on the hearthrug and scratched, with his heavy leg thumping rhythmically on the floor. Tibbles sat beside him, elegantly scratching too. Up on the dresser, Romulus and Remus were scratching as well.

"Drat you!" said Tibbles. "I think you've given me—"

At that moment, Duffie leaned forward and stared incredulously at a small brown something crawling on her wide leg. *"What?"* she said. She caught the small brown thing between her finger and thumb and waved it about. "This," she said dramatically, "is a flea. That Filthy Creature has fleas. Kathleen, if they are not got rid of by bedtime, it goes down to the vet tomorrow. Bathe it. Hoover the living room. And do it at once!"

"Oh dear!" Kathleen jumped up at once. "Yes, Duffie. What in?"

"The bath, of course. And make sure you clean it thoroughly afterwards," said Duffie. "I'll deal with those cats."

"Drat you!" wailed Tibbles, as Duffie snatched her up.

Duffie went on to collect Romulus and Remus too. She held them draped head to head in a bundle and marched off to the kitchen with them. From the sink came dreadful rinsings and desperate yowlings. Sirius, trembling all over, was hauled upstairs by Kathleen and Robin, and Basil actually left his Remains to come and push him from behind. The bath was filled. Sirius backed away from the rising steam, rumbling with terror. He braced his legs. But the whole family seemed to agree with Duffie for once. Mr. Duffield came through the door behind him before he could back himself out through it.

"In you go, horse," Mr. Duffield said.

Sirius, to his terror and acute humiliation, was lifted as if he were a mere cat and plunged into warm water. It was a dreadful experience. He was quite sure it was killing him. Three times he almost got out, and three times the four humans thrust him back in. They were soaked to the skin. Mr. Duffield hit him a number of times, harder every time. But Sirius would rather have been hit than stay in that bath. He struggled in a frantic green rage, his eyes blazing and his teeth bared.

"Good lord, Rat! It's only water," said Basil.

"Leo!" said Kathleen. She was profoundly shocked. She had never seen him look like this before.

Sirius gathered he was upsetting her. He did his best to be less angry, but he was still terrified. He shook all over, until at last they had finished and let go of him. Then he came out of the bath like a sea wave, bringing most of the bath water with him, and fled downstairs, soaking everything on the way. Duffie was in the living room, grimly powdering the struggling cats. She received the rest of the water all over her as Sirius shook himself. The cats fled helter-skelter. Duffie seized the poker and drove Sirius out into the yard, where he crawled into his shelter and crouched shivering. Robin and Kathleen tried to get in after him with bath towels, but he hated being dried as much as he hated the bath. If it had not been Robin and Kathleen, he would have bitten them. He snarled and he growled, and he upset Kathleen completely. She burst into tears.

"She's made Leo hate me. He'll never forgive me. *Listen* to him, Robin!"

The snarling made Robin quite scared, but he said stoutly, "He knows it's not your fault. After all, he could have bitten us." It made him feel better to point that out. It also brought Sirius to his senses and made him deeply ashamed of frightening them. He came shivering out of his shelter and licked them both apologetically. "There! See?" said Robin, and Kathleen hugged Sirius, wet as he was, until she made him grunt.

Then he went indoors and started scratching again.

The bath had done no good at all.

"Powder it," Duffie said frigidly.

Kathleen left off vacuuming, and powdered Sirius till he sneezed. That seemed to do very little good either. Kathleen looked across the room at Duffie's grim face and was really frightened. "What shall we *do?*"

"Try one of those flea collars," Robin suggested. "A boy at school told me they worked like magic."

Next day was the start of the Easter holiday. Kathleen hastened out before Duffie was up and bought a peculiar transparent collar, which she fastened around Sirius's neck alongside his usual one. It smelled of something queer, but he soon grew used to it. And it worked. It would have been hard to say if Kathleen or Sirius was more relieved. Sirius was comfortable again before evening. Duffie told Kathleen that That Creature could stay as long as he wore a flea collar in the future. Kathleen was glad, but she had another worry instead.

"It cost an awful lot," she confessed to Sirius that night. "And I've almost no money of my own left now. My Daddy sent me some money after he first went to jail, but he hasn't sent me any more—I don't think they give them much there —and I don't know how I'm going to feed you, Leo, I really don't. Duffie won't let me buy your food with the housekeeping, and Uncle Harry's fifty pence is just not enough. I shall be all spent up after Easter, and I don't know *what* we'll do."

Sirius knew that he could get food from Miss Smith. He

tried to tell Kathleen he would be all right by making a groaning noise and nosing her hand.

Kathleen understood he was trying to comfort her. "Not to worry, Leo," she said. "I can be cunning and make sure there's scraps. It's dishonest, but we'll manage."

The short time the Easter holiday lasted was rather a thin time for Sirius. He did not dare go out, even to see Miss Smith, in case somebody saw how he got out. The first opportunity he got, he stood on his hind legs and bolted the top bolt on the gate. Tibbles had already bolted the bottom one. She did it every night. After that, he had nothing to do but hang about the house until Kathleen was free to take him for a walk, and to think about food. He was still growing a little, and he seemed to be hungry all the time. He had not intended to bother Kathleen for food, but he did. Whenever she was in the kitchen, he lay on her feet with a flop and a groan, to show her he was dying of hunger. If this did not work, he sat where he could touch her hand with his nose whenever she passed him. And when it was near his suppertime, he followed Kathleen about, staring anxiously at her in case she forgot what time it was.

"Really, Leo, you're like a starving beggar!" said Kathleen. "Do I ever forget now?"

When he was not thinking of food, Sirius worried that Basil would find the Zoi. Clive called for Basil nearly every day, and the two of them went off to hunt for the mysterious meteorite. Sirius tried to make them take him, too. Every time they left, he rushed after them to the door, ears pricked and tail whirling, hoping Basil would melt. But Clive hated dogs. Basil always shut the door in his face, saying, "Get out of it, Rat."

Once, when Kathleen was shaking a mat outside the side door, Sirius managed to push past her and go bounding after the two boys. He thought that once he was with them, Basil might just let him stay. But Clive made irritated noises to cover up a jump of fear. Basil said, "Oh bother you, you festering Rat!" He seized Sirius by his collar and towed him rapidly back to the house. He was in too much of a hurry to go to the side door, so he opened the door of the shop and thrust Sirius inside it. "Don't let the Rat out, Mum. He keeps trying to follow us."

The shop was full of Duffie's usual customers—the loud-voiced ladies in drab clothes who all called her Duffie. Duffie plunged among them and grabbed Sirius's collar. "Blast Basil! Blast the creature! It'll break everything in sight."

"It's a fine-looking animal, Duffie," one of the women boomed.

"Not bad for a mixture," said one with a sharper voice. "What kind of fearsome cross is it, Duffie?"

This voice struck into Sirius's head and brought back a nasty memory. Surely the sharp voice went with a large strong hand that turned you upside down and then said you were not worth keeping alive? He looked up at the woman as Duffie dragged him past. She was a ruddy-faced being in corduroy trousers and heavy boots. She did not look big enough to have turned him upside down. But he was sure she was the one. The doggy smell on her trousers was the same.

"Eleanor Partridge, you're a snob," boomed the booming woman. "Mongrels are always far more intelligent. I like the look of this one. High I.Q., you can see."

Because of this praise, Duffie did not bundle Sirius away quite as fiercely as she might have done. It was Sirius who sped to the house door, towing Duffie.

"I don't like his eyes," said the sharp voice.

Sirius burst through into the living room, bristling. Sacks and suffocation went with that voice. He threw himself at Kathleen, so upset that he tried yet again to communicate with her, and whimpered for sympathy. "Keep it *in*," said Duffie.

"Silly!" said Kathleen. "You know they never take you. Be good now, and we'll go out this afternoon."

Kathleen was having to spring-clean the house. Duffie insisted on it after the flea. Sirius strongly resented it. Kathleen was scraping away layers of calm, familiar dust, and replacing it with uncomfortably clean new smells of polish and disinfectant. It bored him silly, and he knew Kathleen was working far too hard at it. When she took him out at last, she was too tired to do more than sit on the gate to the meadow and throw sticks for him. Sirius resented this so that he did his best at first to stop Kathleen spending the whole day cleaning. He would stand, very patient and obstinate, with his head down and his tail stiffly out, exactly where he was most in the way. "Do get *out*, Leo!" Kathleen kept saying. She vacuumed his tail up twice, by mistake. But

Sirius still stood in her way, until Duffie stormed up and delivered a long lecture on lazy sluts who spent their time playing with useless dogs instead of washing the paint down.

"*Do* get out of the way, Leo," Kathleen said miserably, when Duffie had gone.

After that, Sirius simply followed Kathleen about. He tried to alleviate the boredom of it by exercising the right of a luminary to poke into odd holes and corners. One such corner had a mousetrap in it. That was horrible. He could not get the thing off his nose.

"Curiosity killed the dog!" Kathleen said, running to his rescue. "Poor Leo. No, don't go in there! It's full of moth-balls."

The mothballs were horrible too. They made Sirius feel ill. It was the only day he did not feel hungry. Altogether he did not enjoy that holiday. The only good thing in it was that Basil and Clive did not find the Zoi. Sirius made quite sure of that by examining every heap of muddy fragments Basil brought back. Basil was furious. One evening, when Sirius was sniffing at the finds, Basil kicked him.

"Don't do that!" Mr. Duffield said sharply. "It would serve you right to be bitten." He called Sirius over to him. "Come here, horse." Sirius went over, low and slinking, not at all sure what was going to happen. Last time Mr. Duffield noticed him, he had been plunged in warm water. To his surprise, he got his head rubbed amiably. "You're a most forbearing animal," Mr. Duffield told him, "or I wouldn't keep you. There must be at least two people in this house you'd give your eyes to bite—naming no names. Good dog." Sirius thought this was most perceptive of Mr. Duffield. He wagged his tail heartily.

Just before the holiday ended, Kathleen, to her intense joy, had a letter from her father. It was the first one she had had since Sirius had been living in the house, and it did not strike him as a very good letter. It was written and addressed in smudgy pencil, on paper torn off something larger, and the envelope was very dirty and creased. But Kathleen was evidently so delighted with it that Sirius planted his front paws on her knees and congratulated her.

"Make it go down," said Duffie. "It'll be climbing on the table next. Does this father of yours bother to tell you when he's coming out of prison?"

"Yes!" said Kathleen, joy all over. "He says in a month or so. Fancy!"

"Thank goodness for that," said Duffie. "I'm not a charity. I've enough to do without feeding and clothing Irish children for a year. It's high time that feckless terrorist was made to be responsible for you."

Sirius wished he could point out to Duffie that she would have to do all the housework again if Kathleen left. But he saw that Duffie's unkindness had not spoiled Kathleen's joy. Kathleen was almost too used to Duffie to notice what she said. She took Sirius away upstairs to make the beds and talked to him excitedly.

"You'll love my Daddy when you meet him, Leo. He's ever so sweet and kind and funny, and making jokes all the time. This letter's not really like him. His spelling's terrible. But it's sweet too. He says he'll come and fetch me as soon

as he's free. Just think, Leo! I'll take you, and we'll all
go back to Ireland and live in a house by ourselves. Won't
that be marvelous? Daddy'll love you. I know he will. And
it won't be long now. We've only a month to wait. I can
hardly *believe* it, Leo!"

Sirius sat down in some dismay on a trailing end of
blanket. This was something he had not thought of. Of
course he would go where Kathleen went. And, if he had
not found the Zoi before Kathleen's father came for her,
then he would be taken far away and never would find it.

"Leo!" said Kathleen, tugging.

He realized that she was trying to pull the blanket out
from underneath him and got up dejectedly. Kathleen, as
she tucked in the blanket, heard his feet ticker-tacking away.

"It's all right. I'm not angry," she called. "It's just you
always sit on the thing I need next." But Sirius had his nose
pushed out of the window in the next room, anxiously looking for Sol, and did not hear her.

"Yes, I see the difficulty," Sol said. "I tell you what. Basil
and his friend keep searching upriver, near the place where
you were born. Boys have such a knack of finding things that
I think you should take a look there too. After all, you were
put there first of all."

"If you think I should," Sirius said, without enthusiasm.
Mrs. Partridge went with the place where he was born. And
with her went sacks in the river. He was not at all anxious
to meet Mrs. Partridge again. As soon as Kathleen was back
at school, the first place he went was into town, to batter
at Miss Smith's door.

"School holidays over I see," said Miss Smith. "On your own again all day, are you? Well, come in. I've got quite a bit saved up for you."

She gave him an excellent meal, and they had a splendid reunion. But Sirius knew that the splendid meal was due to the fact that he had not been to visit Miss Smith for nearly three weeks. He was hungry again soon after, and he knew that Kathleen would not have enough food at home for a dog that had been roaming the town all day. The fact was, he told himself, he needed more food than Kathleen and Miss Smith could supply. That was what he told Sol, when Sol asked him why on Earth he was not going upriver. "I'm finding people to feed me," he said. It made a splendid excuse for not going near Mrs. Partridge yet.

Sirius started his career as a beggar by trying to sponge on butchers' shops. He went softly into a shop behind a customer.

"Sorry, madam," said the butcher. "This is a food shop. We don't allow dogs."

"But it's not *my* dog!" said the customer.

Then the butcher and his assistants held the door open and waved at Sirius. "Shoo! Go home! Out!" They were so fierce about it that Sirius had to go. But in the second shop he tried, he sensed a spark of kindness somewhere. He was not sure where the spark was, in the butcher himself or in the customers, but he set to work to fan it. He whined and groveled. He trembled all over, his apologetic tail sweeping the sawdust and his sides sucked in until they nearly met in the middle.

"Poor thing," said the butcher. "He's starving. Give him that chunk of shin, George, and put him out."

Sirius swallowed the meat on the pavement outside and then tried another butcher. And another. His technique improved all the time. He came to see at once, as soon as he entered the shop, who it was had the spark of kindness, and he concentrated on that person. If there was no spark, he left at once. He also discovered that if he put his ears as low as they would go, it made his eyes glow and gave his whole face a soft, appealing look. In the fifth shop, the butcher said, "I call it a shame, letting a lovely dog like that go half starved!"

Sirius went home very satisfied—though he was rather surprised to find he was not particularly interested in the lights Kathleen had bought for him.

The next day, he tried a new method. He went along several streets and, whenever he found a gate he could open, he went inside and boldly battered on the front door of the house. When it was opened, he sat on the doorstep, looking as appealing as he knew how, and wagging just the tip of his tail—ever so hopefully. He was surprised how often the person in the house exclaimed, "Oh, you beauty!" and gave him a biscuit or a cake. Sometimes, of course, there was a dog in the house already. Sirius found it wisest to go away as soon as it barked. Dogs were jealous. Sometimes again, the person who opened the door was frightened of dogs. Sirius learned to detect this as soon as the door was opened. He did not waste time on such people. And then again some people were like Duffie. He met a blast of cold dislike. He left those doorsteps at once, but even so, he got kicked once.

Ranging the streets, always on the alert for providers, Sirius soon found that the best ones usually called to him first. Two old men called to him from seats and shared sandwiches with him. There was another old man called Mr. Gumble who insisted on Sirius going into his house with him, where he gave him a steak. It seemed that Mr. Gumble had just done well at the betting shop on the corner of the street. Sirius could see Mr. Gumble was very poor. Nevertheless, he accepted the steak, and went back to see all three old men next day. They loved feeding him. And he made them happy by being grateful and affectionate.

"You're just finding excuses," said Sol, who was both amused and exasperated by this begging.

"Not really," said Sirius. "They want to make a fuss of something. Why shouldn't it be me?"

"All right," said Sol. "Now go and look upriver."

But before he had gone half a mile in the right direction, Sirius met a bright pink van with a blue cow on top, drawn up near a play school. A very small boy reached toward him with a fistful of cold, sweet, white stuff. Sirius ate it all. And that was that. Having discovered ice cream, Sirius could think of nothing else for a while. He found another pink van and begged at it like an artist. Sol, annoyed though he was, blazed with laughter at the way Sirius sat just a little beyond the queue, pretending to be too timid to go nearer, and yearned in every soulful hair for a drop of ice cream. He got a whole cornet too, from the man who sold it.

"You are shameless!" said Sol. "To think you were once a high effulgent!"

"Pooh!" said Sirius, head down and guzzling, with his tongue rammed into the cornet. "It was worth it."

All the same, he knew he had run out of excuses for not going near Mrs. Partridge. So he set off to see if Bruce had managed to open his gate yet.

But before he came to the end of the street where the hallo-dogs lived, Sirius had forgotten Bruce. He had forgotten Mrs. Partridge, forgotten the Zoi, forgotten Sol, forgotten everything. There was a strong something in the air. It seemed stronger even than a scent. Whatever it was, it tingled worse than the Zoi and drew him on. He could do nothing to resist it. It dragged him down the street, past Rover and Redears. They felt it too. Neither of them said Hallo. Bruce was working at his latch in a frenzy. He did not even notice Sirius.

"The Zoi!" Sol said, unheeded, as Sirius broke into a gallop.

The feeling was coming from Patchie. She was in her yard as usual, looking very charming. Outside her gate was every dog in the neighborhood who could get loose. Sirius wanted to get into that yard. He could think of nothing but getting near Patchie. But the wire fence was high. The Labrador half of Sirius made him a poor, clumsy jumper. He knew he could never get over the fence. So he settled down among the other dogs, as close as he could get to the gate, and forgot everything else.

"Oh well," said Sol. "Dogs will be dogs, I suppose."

9 THE NEXT WEEK or so was the queerest and most upsetting time Sirius had ever experienced. He did not understand what was happening to him. Dog was all over his green nature, swamping it. He knew it was, but he could not help it. He did not know what it was about Patchie which was making him like this. It was not as if he cared about her the way he did for Kathleen or his lost Companion. He did not care two hoots for Patchie herself. Yet he had to go and sit hopelessly outside her gate all and every day, and it was a terrible wrench when he found it was time to leave.

He went thin, and his coat was less glossy. He called hastily on his providers, ate and left. Mr. Gumble did not understand. He was hurt. Miss Smith understood perfectly. "Poor Sirius," she said. "And I expect she's shut up. They usually are, you know."

If Sirius could have asked her what was the matter with him, he would have done. The queer strong feeling was driving him nearly frantic. It was so different from everything he had known before that he did not know how to cope with it. He knew he should be looking for the Zoi, but he could not leave Patchie's gate. At length, he asked the other patiently waiting dogs what was the matter with them all. Most of them had no idea. They only knew they would sit there night and day if they could, until Patchie came out

to them. And she never did. But one hideous old mixture
of a dog, with a head like a grizzly bear's, explained gruffly:

"She's in heat. She could have pups. That's why we're
here."

"Is that it?" Patchie said brightly from beyond the gate.
"I couldn't think why I'd got so many friends all of a sudden.
Hallo, hallo. I love you all!" She was in a very cheerful and
flirtatious mood. "Why don't some of you come in?"

None of the dogs could jump the high wire fence. They
all sighed deeply. It made not a bit of difference to them,
Sirius included, to know why they were waiting. They were
too taken up with the feeling coming from Patchie even to
quarrel over her. They just sat in a group on the pavement,
each one of them panting with excitement, so that from a
short distance the whole group seemed to vibrate like the
engine of an old car.

That week Patchie's owner and Bruce's were knocking
down houses only a couple of streets away. They came
home for a cup of tea. Bruce's owner stood and looked at
the vibrating group, the hanging tongues, the quickly heaving sides and the patient faces.

"Got the usual squad of lovers, I see."

"Yes. I shall be glad when it's over," said Patchie's owner.
He waded among the waiting dogs, pushing them aside, telling them half-heartedly to cut along home, and stopped
when he came to Sirius. "Hey! This is your Bruce got out
again!"

"No, it's not," said Bruce's owner. "And it's not Rover or
Redears either. Must be another one of them."

"Someone must have tried to drown a whole sackful that time," said Patchie's owner. "I wish I could ask this one if he was out of the river too. Here—the gate's unlocked. Come in quick."

In this way, Sirius learned that the hallo-dogs were indeed his brothers and sister. But he was a dog, and the knowledge did not mean as much to him as it might to a human. He was too taken up with Patchie. He made a deft effort to get through the gate with the two men. Bruce's owner caught him by the scruff of his neck and turned him out. So he settled down to hopeless waiting again.

"Leo doesn't look well," Kathleen said anxiously. "Should I take him to a vet?"

"He's all right. He's probably growing again," said Mr. Duffield.

Sirius did not feel well. He felt sick with longing. By the middle of the second week of sitting dumbly panting on the pavement he was nearly in a fever. But that day there was a new dog.

The new dog came trotting up around midday and lay down panting beside the others. A faint chill came off him. Although Patchie was busy most fetchingly scratching one of her fox-red ears, Sirius could not help turning to look at the newcomer. He was large, larger than Sirius, and older. In fact, he was a magnificent dog in the prime of his life. The white hair on his body gleamed like snow in moonlight. The red of his drooping ears was beyond fox-red, beyond chestnut, into blood color, and glowed against the gleaming snow of his body. His eyes were bright cat-like yellow, and the pupils were slits, like a cat's eyes in sunlight.

Sirius stared. He felt the hair coming up along his spine with a feeling that seemed to be excitement. Yet it was nothing like the feeling coming from Patchie. There was fear in it. That had to do with the chill coming off the stranger. He noticed that the other dogs were all moving away a little. But together with the fear and the chill, Sirius felt a faint frosty tingle, a tiny prickle of life much stronger and more serious than anything to do with Patchie. Sirius sat up. He knew that prickle. It came from creatures who had been near a Zoi.

"Who are you?" he said.

The strange dog turned its cat-slit eyes on him for a second, and then looked away. He did not answer. Instead, he lay couchant like a lion, watching Patchie. He watched indulgently, as if he knew Patchie was very young and very silly and that amused him. He did not talk to her either, though she of course said Hallo.

After half an hour of watching, the strange dog seemed to decide that he had lain there long enough. He got up and sauntered a few steps sideways and back, away from the fence. Then he halted. His head moved measuringly. His cat eyes looked from ground to fence and back again. He was clearly considering jumping the fence. Sirius looked at the stranger's long strong legs—which had glistening feathery fringes very like his own—and had no doubt that he could do it too.

Neither had the other dogs. They moved protestingly. The grizzly bear dog said, "I say! That's not fair!"

The strange dog ignored them. He tensed. His yellow eyes stared fixedly at the top of the fence and his legs braced for a leap.

Then came a noise. It was shrill and sweet and seemed to come from very far away. But it felt to Sirius as if it was taking place just between his ears. It was a sound so haunting and imperious that his nose came up and his ears pricked. It seemed to be calling him. The strange dog shook his head and looked irritated. Patchie had heard the sound too. She was sitting with her ears cocked and her head sideways, looking charming. None of the other dogs responded. It seemed that only the three of them—Patchie, Sirius and the stranger—had heard it.

The sound stopped. The strange dog hesitated. He looked at Patchie, sitting looking so charming. And that seemed to decide him. His eyes went to the top of the fence again. His legs bent and lowered him for a jump.

The noise tunneled hauntingly through Sirius's head again. This time, it was longer, louder and more commanding. Feeling he ought to do something about it, Sirius doubtfully stood up. Patchie whined. The strange dog, looking quite exasperated, stood to his proper height again, hesitated a second, and then turned and galloped off up the street.

Sirius raced after him. The stranger went so fast that Sirius had really to stretch himself to catch him, running as he had seldom run before, with his front and back legs jackknifing together and apart, his back arched then straight, arched then straight, and the pads of his paws beating the pavement till they glowed.

"What was that noise?" Bruce called as the two dogs shot past. Beyond Bruce, Redears and Rover were whining as Patchie had done.

Sirius could not spare time to answer. But he registered the fact that all five of them, and only they, apart from the strange dog, could hear the noise. It was one more peculiar thing. His curiosity was thoroughly aroused. The other dog settled to a steady loping. Sirius hung his purpling tongue out as far as it would go and overhauled him grimly. He was close behind as they shot through the dust and noise where the houses were being knocked down. He came up alongside as they reached the raw cindery stretch beyond. They ran shoulder to shoulder across it toward the older cleared space where bright green grass now grew.

"Go away!" said the other dog.

"No," panted Sirius.

They ran on into the ragged green grass. Sirius's paws were thankful for it. When they were in among the first weedy mounds of rubble, the other dog slowed down, stopped and looked irritably at Sirius. Sol was behind a bank of purple cloud. In the dimmer light, the strange dog's coat shone dazzlingly against the green. And, now it was colder and he himself so hot, Sirius could feel the chill off him more strongly than ever.

"I told you to stop following me," said the strange dog. "Are you going, or do I have to bite you?"

Sirius heaved for breath. "I daresay I could bite you back. Who are you?"

The stranger looked at him for a second. Then he casually leaned backwards, stretching his forepaws in front of him so that the muscles in his heavy shoulders rippled. He stood languidly to his full height again, to show Sirius that he was an inch or so larger all around and his bones were thicker and his chest deeper, because he was in his prime. "You think you can bite me?" he said. "Forget it. You've been wasting your strength yearning over that silly girl-puppy. And you hadn't the strength to jump her fence anyway. Come back in two years and bite me then. You still couldn't." He yawned in Sirius's face. Then, as if he was quite sure Sirius would not bother him further, he turned and trotted away.

Sirius bounded after him. "Wait! Who are you? Where do you come from?"

"Leave me alone!" the other said, in a snap across his shoulder as they ran.

"Just tell me where the Zoi is," Sirius panted. They went stride for stride through a patch of newly sprouting nettles. "I know you've been near it. I can feel it on you."

"I don't know what you're talking about."

"You must. It tingles like nettles."

They came to another heap of rubble. The other dog stopped again, gleaming against the dark mound. Behind him, small yellow coltsfoot stood out as bright as luminaries on the earth. "Look—why are you following me around like this? I'm in a hurry."

"I know you are," said Sirius. "I heard the whistle. But that doesn't stop you telling me who you are, and why you look like me, and where the Zoi is."

The strange dog's arrogant eyes swept over Sirius. His cat's pupils were wider because of the dim light, but still not very wide. Sirius felt the coat on his back mounting a little. Those eyes were truly unearthly. The stranger saw it, and rumbled a low, contemptuous growl. "So you heard him whistling for me? I suppose that must mean you're a half-breed relation of ours. We go out and about sometimes. But I don't see why I should tell red and yellow puppies anything about us. Go away, mongrel. I warned you!"

Sirius lost his temper. No creature had any right to take that tone with him. A growl was rumbling in his throat from the moment he was called a half-breed. It grew and grew, and Sirius's anger grew and throbbed with it. His ears rose. The hair on his back piled itself into a long crest. Every white tooth in his head bared itself. And suddenly, from that, he lit to a great green rage. The green light of his fury made two lurid spots on his enemy's white coat. The strength of a luminary lit him from inside, and he knew he could make red steaks of this arrogant creature.

The other dog was terrified. He had never seen anything like this, and he was used to being the unearthly one. But he had been bred for bravery and he had his pride. His yellow eyes glared into Sirius's green blazing ones. He, too, bared his teeth and backed, snarling, up the mound to give himself the advantage. With an effort, he got his back up and his tail stiffly curved above it. He was large and strong and menacing, but he was scared nearly silly.

Sirius knew he was. His green rage fired further with the joy of victory coming. He sprang. There was hoarse howling, baying, and the click of snapping teeth. Their two yelling heads dodged, parried, dived and snatched. Sirius struck like a snake at his enemy's throat. The other dog yelped, knowing it was the winning stroke, and tried to stumble sideways.

Then the queer noise came for a third time, almost as if the strange dog's unseen master knew. It was a haunting torment in both their heads. The strange dog could not move. Sirius could barely think for the sound. But he was still in such a green rage that he managed to close his mouth on his enemy's cold throat. When the sound stopped, he had him pinned firmly, not in a fighting grip, but so that he could not get away.

"Let me go!" said the other dog, tugging sideways and back. "He's whistled three times now. I have to go."

The queer coldness of the strange dog's coat made Sirius's mouth numb. He could hardly tell where his teeth were. "No. Tell me who you are and where the Zoi is."

"I've never *seen* your beastly Zoi! And I can't tell you anything about us or our Master. Only those who run with us and share our duties are allowed to know. My name's Yeff. That's all I can tell you. Now *let me go!*"

Yeff seemed quite frantic. He tugged until Sirius was afraid he would rip his throat, and, since Sirius's mouth was now so numb that he could not tell how hard he was biting, he thought he had better loosen his grip a little. As soon as he did, Yeff jerked his jowl loose and ran away up the mound in great fluid leaps.

Sirius scrambled after him, heavy, clumsy and tired.

Nevertheless, he was not far behind as Yeff leaped from the top of the mound and down the other side. Sirius reached the top only a second later. There was no sign of Yeff. The cleared space went on behind the mound, level here and sprouting green things, for fifty yards or so, but it was utterly empty. Yeff was gone. If he had melted like the snow his coat resembled, he could not have vanished more completely.

Sirius hung his numbed tongue out of his cold, aching mouth and stared. Here was yet another mystery. And his one contact with the Zoi had gone. He could have flung his head back and howled. He looked up, hoping that Sol might have seen where Yeff went. Sol, however, was still under purple clouds. They had been spitting rain as Sirius ran up the mound. Now they poured in earnest, cold and stinging rain, hammering on the rubble and fizzing on the cinders. It was April, after all. But Sirius was fairly sure Sol was annoyed with him for wasting his time outside Patchie's gate. He was seeing what cold water would do.

Sirius hated rain almost as much as he had hated that bath. He turned and ran. The spell Patchie had cast on him was broken anyway. Meeting Yeff had done that. As he ran, he cursed himself for losing Yeff, for annoying him in the first place, for going and losing his temper—for the whole thing. And he had such a short time before Kathleen carried him off to Ireland. Soaked, wretched and worn out, he climbed the steps to Miss Smith's front door and battered on it in the place where he had already made quite a mark.

"I was just going to have my rest," Miss Smith said, looking down at him. "My poor dog! What dripping misery! Come in at once. No—not in the kitchen. Shake in the hall where it doesn't show. Do you like being rubbed with a towel? No? Very well, I shall put the towel on this chair." Sirius, shivering, watched Miss Smith spread a large white towel on a shabby armchair. "This was Lass's favorite chair," she told him. "I think you'll find it comfortable. It must be a better shape for dogs than it is for humans. Now you get into it and sleep off whatever it is that happened, and I'll put the electric fire here so it will dry you off. Don't knock it, will you? And don't disturb me for an hour or so, there's a kind dog. I have to have my rest because these days I don't sleep so well at night."

Gratefully, Sirius climbed into the chair. It was a perfect fit. He thumped his tail and fell asleep, dripping gently on the threadbare carpet, while rain hammered and trickled on the windows of Miss Smith's house.

About a quarter to four, the rain stopped. Sirius started up. He knew at once it was late. The clouds were so low and heavy still that he could not tell how late. He came out of the chair and whined. The house was quiet, except for Miss Smith's noisy little clock which would only work lying on its face. He went out into the dark hall and tried to open the front door. But it had a round handle and he could not manage it. There was only one thing for it. He went, rather diffidently, upstairs to look for Miss Smith.

She was lying on the bed in the first room he came to, fast asleep and snoring a little, looking so tranquil that it seemed a shame to wake her. But Sirius did not know what else to do. He went and pushed his cold nose gently against her soft, wrinkled cheek. Miss Smith gave a little gasp and opened her eyes.

"Oh, it's not Lass, of course! It's Sirius. My dear, I'm sorry. I've been asleep for hours. It felt so peaceful with a dog in the house again. But you want to go, don't you? I'm afraid I'm too sleepy to get up—so I'll tell you a secret, Sirius. If you go into the kitchen and push the bottom of the back door, you'll find it opens. It's a dog-door I had made for Lass. And I'm sure a clever dog like you can manage the garden gate. Just tread on the latch, Sirius. It has a spring to close it."

Sirius gently nosed his thanks to her and hurried away downstairs. Just as Miss Smith had said, the back door and the garden gate conveniently opened. He wished everyone was as understanding as Miss Smith.

Miss Smith lay back on her pillow, anxiously listening to his progress. She smiled when she heard the garden gate click. "Understood every word. I thought he would, bless him. But it looks late. He'll be in trouble. If he doesn't turn up tomorrow, I'll know they've found he can get out."

10

SIRIUS WENT HOME at a hasty canter. He knew as soon as he was outside that it was not quite as late as he had thought. But it was late enough. He had barely time to get back before Kathleen did. He galloped around the corner into the right street, almost skidding in his hurry, and found he was actually behind Kathleen. She was halfway up the street. He could get there. If he dived into the side street that led to the lane behind the yard, he could be in the yard with the gate shut and his collar on, and Kathleen would never know he had been out.

But Kathleen was in trouble. He could see she was. There was a gang of boys all around her, shouting things, and one kept trying to pull her hair. The sight of Kathleen being pushed and jostled all over the pavement was more than Sirius could take. He could not help it if he was found out. He trotted forward with his ears pricked to see what he could do.

There were six boys of several sizes. They were pinching and shoving Kathleen, and stamping in puddles so that she was showered with muddy water. Sirius could see from Kathleen's face that this had often happened to her and she had no way of stopping it.

"What's at the bottom of an Irish milk bottle?" shrieked the smallest boy, who seemed to be Kathleen's chief tormentor.

"Open other end!" roared the others, screaming with laughter and shoving Kathleen this way and that.

"How do you brainwash an Irishwoman?" yelled the first boy.

"Fill her boots with water!" screamed the others, stamping in puddles for all they were worth.

Sirius's trot dropped to a crouching walk. He crept forward, growling softly. Perhaps it was the misery on Kathleen's face, or perhaps it was that he had already lost his temper once that day, but he became angrier with every step. Too bad it was the smallest boy who was the worst. Sirius's growl became a snarl. The boys were too busy shouting to hear him. As the smallest boy opened his mouth to ask what they put at the top of Irish ladders, Sirius lit to a green rage again and sprang.

The boys found themselves barged aside by something they thought was a raging lion. Its eyes blazed like green torches. It hit the smallest boy in the chest and knocked him over backwards. Then it stood on him, snarling, baring a set of huge white teeth and making his terrified face green with the light from its eyes.

"*Leo!*" said Kathleen. It was half relief, half reproach, and very wobbly.

Sirius knew he must not upset her any further. He had to content himself with snarling around the ring of boys. Two green beams from his eyes flitted over them all. He was trying so hard not to bite the boy he was treading on that foam dripped across his bared teeth and down from his open jaws. The boys backed away hurriedly. One of them slipped on the rainy pavement and sat down. Sirius hoped it hurt him.

"Go away," Kathleen said shakily. "Leave me be, or I'll set my dog on all of you."

"Call that a dog!" said one of the boys. "That's a beeping monster!"

Sirius stepped off the smallest boy and crawled slowly at the rest, growling ardently. They did not wait for him to reach them. Those on their feet ran. The other two scrambled up and pelted after them. Sirius bounded behind, his eyes blazing, blown up to twice his real size, barking as horribly as he knew how.

When he had chased them to the end of the street, he heard three voices calling him. "Leo! *Shamus!* RAT!" Reluctantly, Sirius left the chase and came trotting back. His coat settled down as he came, and by the time he reached Kathleen, his eyes were their normal green. Basil and Robin were with Kathleen.

"How did he get out?" Basil demanded.

"I don't know," Kathleen said shakily. "He—he was just there suddenly." Sirius could see she was trying not to cry. He tried to go and comfort her, but Basil stopped him and rubbed his ears.

"You're quite a good dog really," he said.

"Yes, but we must get him in before Mum finds out," Robin said.

The others anxiously agreed. They hurried Sirius in through the side door and left him in the living room while they all rushed out into the yard to see what had happened there. Tibbles was curled up on the sofa and looked up in surprise.

"You haven't bolted the gate yet, have you?" Sirius asked her.

"Of course not," she said. "You weren't in. What's happened? Did they find you in the road?"

"More or less," said Sirius.

"Then I expect they'll bolt the gate for us," Tibbles said placidly and settled down to sleep again.

"Don't go to sleep," said Sirius. "I need to ask you— Those dogs, the ones Kathleen read about that are white with red ears—where do they come from?"

"Oh," said Tibbles. "Them. I keep out of their way. They don't usually hurt warm beasts like us. They mostly come out at night."

"Where have you seen them?"

Before Tibbles could answer, Basil, Robin and Kathleen came back, loudly wondering who could have opened the yard gate. Kathleen was carrying Sirius's collar. She took him away from Tibbles and pushed the collar firmly over his head.

"That was bad, Leo," she told him.

"He slipped his collar. That's obvious," Basil kept saying. "But someone must have undone the gate for him. Who was it?"

Robin's opinion was that it had been burglars. "Mum keeps clay and glaze and things in the shed. Could they have been after that?"

"Don't be an idiot!" said Basil. "Who wants clay? And

hold your tongue unless we find something's missing."

"You hold yours," Robin retorted.

Neither of them did. They continued to discuss it whenever Duffie was not within hearing. Kathleen set about making supper. She was so pale and shaky still that Sirius kept close beside her, trying to comfort her. He hoped, very earnestly, that it would remain an unsolved mystery who had opened the gate. He hoped Basil and Robin would forget about it soon.

Fate was against him. Later that evening, when the family was sitting around the television, there was a heavy knock at the side door. Basil went to answer it and came back looking very dismayed, and a strange man and a policeman came after him. It seemed that the boy Sirius had knocked over and the one who had sat down were brothers. When they were asked to explain their muddy clothes, they told their father that Kathleen had set a savage dog on them, which had bitten them and mauled them. The strange man was their father. He had gone to the police, and the policeman had come to investigate.

Kathleen said, "He did *not* bite them!" and burst into tears. Duffie looked at her, coldly and triumphantly, and then at Sirius. Sirius quailed. He had a sudden hopeless green memory of being on trial for his life. He felt quite as sick now.

"I think there must be some mistake," said Mr. Duffield. "This dog *never* bites. He's a most forbearing animal, or I wouldn't keep him. And he spends all day tied up in the yard."

"Is this the animal?" said the policeman. "Not much of a house dog, is he, sir? I didn't hear him bark."

"He never barks either," said Mr. Duffield. "That's his other virtue."

The policeman looked as if he did not think it was a virtue. Robin, who knew that it was usually the silent dogs that bit people, and suspected that the policeman knew it too, said quickly, "He's used to people coming in and out of the shop, you see."

"Ah," said the policeman. "Is that it? Perhaps the little girl would give us her version of the episode."

Kathleen could not speak for crying. She was afraid Leo was in mortal danger, and she knew he had looked very savage indeed. It had horrified her. And she could not bring herself to tell anyone how miserable those boys made her, day after day, and how relieved she had been to see Leo.

"There isn't another version," said the father angrily. "This girl set that great brute on my two lads. Ruined their clothes! The wife's furious. It was a huge creature like a lion, they said, all fangs, with green eyes that lit up from inside. Are you sure that's the dog?"

Everyone looked at Sirius. He wagged his tail bashfully and did his best to frown, so that his eyebrows shaded his eyes a little. "Well, his eyes are a sort of green," the policeman said.

"It's the only dog we've got," Duffie said icily. "It's the one you want all right."

"Perhaps we could have your side of the story first," the policeman said to Kathleen. But Kathleen still could not speak. "Anyone else here see anything?" asked the policeman.

Robin and Basil wriggled uncomfortably. They knew they had stood on the other side of the road letting a mere dog come to Kathleen's rescue. Because Robin was the smaller, he was less ashamed than Basil. "Yes," he blurted out. "I was across the road. There were six boys, all onto Kathleen, hitting her and calling names and things."

"My boys wouldn't do that," said the father. "What had *she* done to them?"

"Nothing," sobbed Kathleen. "They always do it."

"Yes. I've seen them nearly every day," Robin said, and then went scarlet because of the way Mr. Duffield was looking at him. "I told you, I was across the road," he said.

"Were you too far away to hear what the—er—argument might have been about?" asked the policeman.

By this time, Basil's face was mottled with shame. "No. We heard them. They were jeering at Kathleen for being Irish." He went even more mottled, remembering how often he had done the same, but he went on, "And the Ra—er— the dog *didn't* bite them. Kathleen didn't even call him. He just came charging up and—er—defended her."

"Irish, eh?" said the policeman.

"My lads take after me," said the father. "I can't abide the Irish."

The policeman coughed. "I have to remind you that there are Race Relations laws, sir."

For a moment the father looked very blank. But he soon rallied. "That's got nothing to do with it. This dog is a dangerous brute that savaged my two lads. It ought to be put down."

"How I agree!" said Duffie.

"He didn't savage them!" said Basil. "He just growled at them and scared them off." Sirius felt that he had never appreciated Basil properly.

"Let's see how fierce he is," the policeman suggested. Sirius was thankful he understood, for, when the policeman suddenly aimed a great punch at him, right between the eyes, he was enough prepared only to blink and back away. The policeman's fist stopped before it reached him. Sirius showed him how mild he was by getting up then, wagging his tail and apologizing to the policeman for being hit by him. "Not what I'd call fierce," said the policeman, rubbing his ears. "Lovely coat he's got." Sirius began to hope that it would not take much more to have the policeman entirely on his side.

The father perhaps thought so too. "What about those blazing eyes?" he demanded aggressively. "My lads said they were like torches. They saw two spots of light coming from them. Now that's not natural."

"Of course it's not natural," said Basil. "It's not true."

"Boys do have a way of exaggerating," the policeman said, seeing the father glaring at Basil. "All I can say is that they're not blazing now." He stood up. "But the police have had one complaint about this dog," he said formally. "I'm bound to tell you that we'll have to take action if we have another."

"Don't worry," said Duffie. "I'll see to it tomorrow."

"Oh, there's no need to do anything now, Madam," the policeman told her. "I was just warning you. I know there's no harm in this dog. He's as playful as a great puppy. He once had me and our driver and His Worship the Mayor and the Town Clerk and goodness knows who-all running chasing him down the High Street. And he thought we were playing with him."

Everyone was astounded. "When on earth was this?" said Mr. Duffield.

"Couple of months ago, it would be," said the policeman.

Then the fat was in the fire. Everyone knew Sirius should have been in the yard. Kathleen sobbed heavily. Duffie rounded on Basil and Basil was forced to admit that the bolts of the yard gate had been undone that evening.

"Well!" said Duffie. "I'm used to Kathleen being sly and underhand. I expect it. But you! I'm ashamed. And anyone could have broken in and taken anything!"

The father began to look smug, as he saw a case might be building up against Kathleen and her fierce brute after all. "That girl drew the bolts," he said.

"I'm sure she did," said Duffie.

"I didn't, I swear," sobbed Kathleen. "On the Holy Bible."

"Then the brute did it himself," said the father. "You see dogs on telly that can open gates. You take him out there. You see."

So everyone trooped out into the yard. The policeman shone his torch on the gate and Sirius was invited to draw back the bolts. Romulus, Remus and Tibbles gathered anxiously on the wall to watch. And Sirius put on a performance beside which his begging was nothing. He was all stupid anxiety to please. He bounced about. He wagged his tail and pricked up his ears willingly. But when Mr. Duffield tried to show him what was wanted by pushing the top bolt backwards and forwards, Sirius became an excited moron. Rover or Redears would have seemed masterminds beside him. It was obviously quite beyond his powers to open anything. They did, with much coaxing, get him to stand on his hind legs and lean his front paws on the gate, but he heaved up with such an effort, so far off the bolt, and looked so idiotically pleased with himself for getting there, that it was clear to everyone that he had never done such a thing in his life before.

"So it looks like somebody opened the gate for him," said the policeman.

"Kathleen," said Duffie's cold voice in the background.

"Don't talk nonsense," said Mr. Duffield. "It was more likely to have been those malicious boys."

"Who are you calling malicious?" the father demanded angrily.

"We'll keep an eye on the place," the policeman said soothingly. "If we see anyone behaving suspiciously, we'll investigate. Otherwise, that seems to be all. But do make sure this dog is properly shut up in future, sir."

The policeman and the father left, but it was not exactly all. While Sirius flung himself down on the hearthrug, thoroughly exhausted with his efforts, Mr. Duffield made Duffie sulk by saying he was sure Kathleen had not unlocked the gate, and that no one could blame the horse for going to her rescue. Then he made Kathleen cry again by demanding to know why she had not told him about the boys. The answer was that Mr. Duffield would not have listened, but Kathleen could not tell him that. After that, Mr. Duffield turned to Basil and Robin and gave them a long lecture on the paltry way they had stood on the other side of the road letting Kathleen be bullied. Kathleen was so embarrassed that she fled to the kitchen. Robin cried. Basil went as sulky as Duffie and muttered that there were six of the festering boys, and he didn't care for the festering Irish either. "I wouldn't have said a word if the Rat hadn't been in trouble," he growled. "That's the last time I do anything for the festering dog!"

Sirius sighed as he heaved off the hearthrug and pattered to the kitchen after Kathleen. Mr. Duffield meant well. But he was too wrapped up in himself to attend to what other people felt. It took a policeman to make him notice anything was wrong, and now he seemed to be making matters worse. He was the most self-centered creature Sirius knew—apart from Duffie, of course.

He found Duffie had cornered Kathleen in the kitchen and was working off some of her bad temper by stumping around the room lecturing her. Kathleen was silent and tear-stained. Sirius went and pressed himself against her and tried to keep his eyes off Duffie's fat hairy calves as they stumped back and forth.

Duffie concluded her lecture after twenty minutes. "I've put up with you and I've put up with That Creature," she ended. "And you reward me by letting it out to savage innocent children. Well, I warn you, Kathleen, this is the last time it does. If I ever find it out again, it goes." By this time Sirius was shaking all over because he so much wanted to take a piece out of one of those stumping calves. "You may well tremble!" Duffie said, pointing at him. "You've run your course. One more thing—one more!—and I take you down to the vet."

Kathleen had stopped crying by bedtime. But she did not play or read. She sat up in bed hugging Sirius.

"Leo," she whispered, "please don't open that gate again. I know it's boring in the yard, but please don't. I know it was you opened it. You're much cleverer than you pretend. But if Duffie takes you to the vet, I won't be able to *bear* it." She squeezed Sirius until he wanted to wriggle free. "Oh, how I *wish* we didn't have to live with the Duffields!" she said.

Sirius had never heard Kathleen admit this before. If he had needed anything more to show him how serious the trouble was, this was it. He licked her face, very kindly, and Kathleen hugged him harder than ever.

The next day, he knew he had to be very careful. As he sat in the yard at the end of his rope, Duffie actually came out of the house three times to make sure that he was there. She seemed disappointed when he was.

"I daren't go out," he said to Sol. "What can I do?"

"That's a pity," said Sol. "She'll get tired of watching you in the end, but I'm afraid you haven't got much time left. Things are happening in Ireland. And the longer you leave that Zoi, the more certain it is the wrong people will find it. And I can't have that. It's done enough damage here as it is. I want you to go and look upriver."

Sirius felt it was good of Sol not to reproach him for wasting his time when he could get out of the yard. "If you really think the Zoi *is* there—" he said. "But I'm not sure. Tell me about white dogs with red ears—cold dogs."

"Those?" said Sol. The fierce bluish color at the very heart of him spread, so that he blazed somber and formidable. "I've nothing against the dogs," he said. "You were bred from one of them—did you know? But their Master is a dark thing. He's one of those I wouldn't like to see getting hold of the Zoi. Listen, I'll give your Duffie something else to think about, if you promise to go and look upriver as soon as you're out."

Sirius shivered. He did not like to say that he suspected that a dark thing had already got hold of the Zoi. He gave another shiver at the thought of Mrs. Partridge. "All right. I promise."

"Thank you," said Sol. "Be patient a day or so."

Patient! thought Sirius. When Sol said time was short, it was. When the Zoi was probably in the wrong hands, and he had found a clue to it, and lost it, when he was tied to this yard, when Kathleen was miserable, how *could* he be patient? He missed roaming about. He wanted to see Miss Smith, Mr. Gumble and his other providers. He lay and thought of ice cream. He was horribly hungry.

"You *do* get hungry," Remus said sympathetically, "if you're used to going hunting. I remember the time I got shut in the bathroom."

The cats put their heads together. In the early afternoon, Romulus trotted along the wall and jumped down onto the roof of the shelter, carrying a mouse. "Here you are," he said kindly. "Let it run about a bit before you eat it. They taste sweeter like that. But I shouldn't eat the tail. That's stringy."

He leaped away again, leaving Sirius staring at a tiny terrified creature crouching between his big blunt paws. He moved his right paw a little. The mouse ran backwards and forwards, squealing with fear. Sirius nosed it. It did not smell very edible and it squealed worse than ever. He knew he could not eat it. He was not used to having his food alive and horrified. But he did not want to offend the cats.

"Run away, you silly thing," he told the mouse. "I'm not going to eat you."

The mouse was insane with fear and did not understand. Sirius looked around all the walls and roofs to make sure none of the cats was around. Then he pushed and nosed the mouse into the far corner of his shelter, where it crouched for the rest of the afternoon, too terrified to move. Kathleen found it when she came to untie Sirius. She picked it up and put it gently inside the shed where Duffie kept her clay.

"Stay there, or the cats will find you," she said to it. The mouse did not understand her either, but it did not appear again.

"I ate the tail," Sirius told Romulus. "It was quite tasty.

Thanks very much." He made do with half a tin of dog food and the scraps from supper that night, and for the rest of the week. It made him mournful. But he was glad that Kathleen seemed happier. As far as he could tell, the boys were not daring to bother her again.

That weekend, to his dismay, Clive called for Basil and they went to look for the Zoi again. They went upriver, and they took Robin to carry the sandwiches. Robin was so proud and flattered to be taken that when they came home that evening, he was talking of collecting Remains for himself. Basil and Clive had not found the Zoi. But they had some Roman oyster shells, a modern clam, a flint that looked almost like an arrowhead, and a bone Basil rather thought was part of an ichthyosaurus. Sirius sniffed it. It smelled of mutton.

Basil clouted him. "Get out, Rat! I'll tell the police on you."

"Please!" Kathleen said. This was a very tender point with her.

"The trouble with you is that you'll believe anything," said Basil.

Over the weekend, something strange happened to the pots Duffie had in her shop window. There had been an artistic stack of them. But, on the side the sun struck them, the glaze had melted and run, and the clay underneath crumbled away. What Duffie found in the window on Sunday evening was a something like a honeycomb, made of twenty half-pots stuck together with glaze. She brought it into the house and waved it dramatically. She tramped about with it, raging. She raged at the glaze-makers. She wagged the honeycomb in people's faces and raged at the clay suppliers. She would have liked to rage at Kathleen and Sirius too. They tried to keep out of her way. She raged instead at shoddy modern products.

"It seems to me that you might as well blame the sunlight, while you're at it," Mr. Duffield remarked from behind the Sunday paper.

Sirius opened his mouth and lolled out his tongue in a wide grin. On Monday morning, he asked Sol how he had done it.

Sol beamed. "A concentration of the right particles. But you can go out now. I can see her through the window making new pots. And I've made sure of a spell of good fine weather, because that usually brings her a shopful of customers. She's not likely to think of you much today."

Joyfully Sirius stood up, dragged the collar off over his ears and drew back the bolts on the gate.

11 MISS SMITH WAS delighted to see him. "I was afraid you'd got yourself shut up for good," she said. She gave him a bowl of raw hamburger. Mr. Gumble gave him a bone and a doughnut. The two old men on the benches gave him a steak pie and a hamburger.

Feeling full and contented, Sirius trotted through the sun-shine to the cleared space where Yeff had vanished. He told himself he was not putting off Mrs. Partridge: he had to check on this place first.

There was not the faintest prickle from the Zoi. But he hardly knew the cleared space, it had changed so in the last week. It was now the beginning of May. The grass was thick and green. The bushes were putting out leaves and the nettles had come up high enough to brush him underneath. The greening mounds of rubble were so studded with dandelions that Sirius felt homesick. The flowers looked like luminaries, and the green was like his own sphere. Earth was a beautiful place.

He was so homesick he thought he would go and see Patchie. He was not sure why, except that he was sad and joyful at once, and it seemed to fit.

As soon as he came to the end of her street, he knew that the compulsive feeling connected with Patchie had gone. There was no longer a crowd of dogs at her gate. "Hallo, hallo!" said Rover and Redears as he trotted by. Bruce was very busy tugging at the latch of his gate with his teeth.

"I've nearly got the hang of this," he said. "I'm working on a new system. You'll see—I'll be out and about like you soon."

"Great!" said Sirius. He trotted on to Patchie's gate and put his nose to the netting. Patchie did not seem to see him. She was scratching nonchalantly. "Hallo," Sirius said.

Patchie looked round. Seeing him, she stood up, stiff-legged and bristling. "Go away. I don't want you."

Very hurt and surprised, Sirius said, "I only came to see how you were."

Patchie let out a rasping growl and advanced on the netting. "Go away. I don't like you. I don't want you. Take your nose away or I'll snap it off."

More hurt and surprised than ever, Sirius moved his nose. "What's wrong? You liked me last week."

"No I didn't. You've got horrid eyes. I don't like anyone except Rover."

"Rover!" exclaimed Sirius, deeply wounded. "He's stupid."

"And you're worse," said Patchie, "thinking I'd like *you!* Go away."

Sirius got up and crept away, pursued by snarls from Patchie. He had never felt so hurt or so mortified before. He could not bring himself to face the other three dogs again. He went the other way, down to the filthy gray-green river, and plodded dejectedly along the towpath with his head down and his tail hanging.

"Cheer up," said Sol. "They often go like that when they come off heat. And she always did like Rover best."

Sirius turned and snarled at him over his shoulder. "Oh, shut up!"

Sol answered with a glare that would have blinded any other creature. "Stop that! You don't even like her. You know she's silly, even for a dog."

There was truth in that. "Yes," Sirius said morosely. "Yes. I suppose you're right."

"I am," said Sol. "Now are you going out toward those

kennels, or do I have to arrange to have you delivered there?"

"All right, all right," said Sirius. "I'll go. There's no point in anything anyway."

He turned and followed the towpath in the other direction. At first he plodded. The river was dirty and depressing. Small smelly factories sat on its banks making it filthier. After those were the railway lines. Sirius walked a little faster. Ever since he had first seen them, he had been interested in the long clattering trains. The railway gave way to allotments, where the black hedges were spattered with bright green buds. Sirius began to feel more cheerful. He trotted. Then he loped. And suddenly he was out in his own meadow where Kathleen took him for walks. It was all blazing green, with dandelions and daisies thicker than the stars of home. Here the river was soft clear blue, a rival to the Milky Way, and the hawthorns on its banks were a piercing young green, as if they had been newly lit with green fire.

Sirius bounded forward jovially. He forgot his hurt pride and frolicked along by the river, around a couple of bends, under tall trees of black lace and yellow-green flames of leaf, until he came to a meadow where there were few flowers but an interesting smell of dog. The dog smell led him up the meadow and through a gate in a newly lit hedge. Here were concrete paths. He dimly remembered that concrete. It led in crisscrosses around low buildings with wire-netting runs in front of them.

He stopped near the center of the crisscrossings and

sniffed the air. There was no Zoi. He was sure Sol was wrong. It was not here. There was dog, however. Dog upon dog, everywhere. And human. A very strong smell of Mrs. Partridge. Sirius hated it. His back rose slightly. There was another smell too, like a mixture of jasmine and ozone. For some reason, it was hauntingly familiar, but Sirius could not place it. All he could tell was that it did not quite fit in with the other smells, the grass, the concrete, the dog, or the Mrs. Partridge. He puzzled about it while he thoughtfully went over and lifted a leg at the corner of the nearest wire run. The smell could have had a tingle of Zoi about it. Or could it? He was not sure.

The dog inside the run hurried over to sniff. "Good morning," she said pleasantly. "I'm Bess."

She was a beautiful yellow-white Labrador with a bright black nose and melting brown eyes. Her sole fault was that she was a trifle stout.

"It is a nice morning," Sirius agreed. He liked the look of this Labrador. He took to her so much, in fact, that he asked, "I say, you don't happen to have seen the thing I'm looking for, do you? It fell out of the sky with a bang some time last year, and it must have looked quite bright as it fell. You know it if you're near it by a strange prickly feeling it gives you."

"Now there you have me," said the Labrador. She sat on her haunches and put her head on one side to think. "I think I know the thing you mean—"

Sirius's ears came up. He could hardly believe them. He wished he had taken Sol's advice earlier. "Go on," he said.

"I saw it come down," said Bess. "It was in the night. I think I must have been going to have puppies, because I felt awfully heavy and miserable, and I went outside to have a good moan at the Moon. And the thing came down past the Moon like—well, I thought it was a star coming unstuck and I was scared stiff. The ground jiggled. But I didn't feel it prickle. It was too far away."

"Thanks," said Sirius. "That's a great help. *How* far away?"

"Down the river, where all those houses are," the Labrador said. "I remember seeing it go into the glare from all their lights just before the ground jiggled."

"So it *is* in the town!" said Sirius. "I wish I'd met you before this. You've been more help than anyone."

"I like to be useful," Bess said, a little wistfully. "I used to be a gun dog until I was sold to Mrs. Partridge. I don't seem much use here."

"Boring, isn't it?" Sirius said feelingly.

"Oh it *is!*" she said. "I see you know, too. Are you a hunting dog, by any chance?"

"Well—only a Zoi-hunter," said Sirius. "Why?"

"You look a bit like a frosty sort of dog that jumped my fence once," said Bess. "Mrs. Partridge didn't have all these high wire things then, so he came over quite easily. He told me he hunted."

"Did he tell you where he came from?" Sirius asked eagerly.

"He was called Yeff," said Bess. "And—"

"Sirius!" said Sol sharply. *"Sirius!"* Light twinkled and

blazed on the wire between the dogs, so that the Labrador backed away blinking. "Run!" said Sol. "Get out of here. Not the way you came—the other direction. Quick!"

Sirius, quite confused, started off the wrong way, found Sol blazing in his eyes and turned back. "Why? What's the matter?"

"It's my fault," said Sol. "I've slipped up again. I've not had much experience recognizing— Just run. Please!"

Since Sol was so urgent, Sirius set off loping toward the next concrete crossroad. He had gone ten feet when Mrs. Partridge came clopping around the corner. Sirius skidded to a stop, turned and bolted the other way.

"Hi!" bawled Mrs. Partridge. "You wretched mongrel! Stop him, Mrs. Canning dear, please!"

Sirius tore back past the Labrador's run, ears flying, tail outstretched, and galloped around the corner. And stopped as if he had run into a wall.

There was another woman standing there, a more elegantly dressed one. She was small, and she had extraordinary dead white hair falling smoothly to her shoulders. Despite that, she seemed young. Her face was dead white too, with cheekbones and eyes that, ever so slightly, slanted upward. That made her both striking and beautiful. The ozone-jasmine scent which had so puzzled Sirius was coming from her—and he knew now that it was a scent quite alien to Earth. Though he had never seen her look quite like this before, he knew her by the faint white nimbus standing around her. He would have known her whatever she looked like.

Sirius wanted to wag his tail and whine with joy. He wanted to go down on his fringed elbows and lick her elegant feet, and then put his paws on her small shoulders and lick her slanting face. But he did nothing. He just stood there, for agelong seconds, staring at her, unable to credit what all his green nature and his dog nature had learned while he had been on Earth. He had met people like her while he begged at doors. One of them had kicked him. He knew Duffie. But she could not be like Duffie! She was his Companion.

His Companion thought he was simply a dog at first. She looked at him with cold dislike, which hurt him, even so, far more than Patchie had done. Sirius knew he should go before she learned he was anything more. But he was too confounded by knowing it to move. Then his Companion looked at his eyes.

"I can't believe it!" she said. Duffie at her coldest and highest was nothing to the way she said it. *"You!* I thought I'd made her have you drowned!" The white nimbus round her spread into a cold blaze. *"You—!"*

The dog nature reacted like lightning, while Sirius's green nature still lay shattered. He jumped clear, back and sideways. Wire netting twanged. His Companion's blast of white hatred lashed the path where he had been standing, consuming dust, setting fire to the grass at the edge, destroying some of the concrete too. Sirius felt the longer hairs of his coat sizzle while he was in the air. He bounced, blundering, into the netting and let it shoot him away again through the chemical reek of the blast, so that he landed on the hot concrete just as his Companion turned and struck the netting where he had been. That blast melted the netting as if it were a nylon stocking, and left it steaming, dripping and turning from dull red to cindery black. Poor Bess howled and ran into the farthest corner. Howling and barking arose from most of the other runs. Sirius had time to see that the Labrador was safe as he ran like a dog possessed, back around the corner of her run and full tilt toward Mrs. Partridge.

Mrs. Partridge had noticed nothing peculiar, beyond an odd smell. She planted her corduroy legs wide across the path to stop Sirius. She did not matter anymore. He went straight between her legs like an arrow. How he made himself low enough he never knew. Mrs. Partridge staggered about. "Wretched brute!" she yelled.

Sirius heard her boots cloppering on the concrete behind him. He heard the small light feet of his Companion overtake them and patter swiftly after him. She might be in human form, but Sirius knew she would run with unearthly speed. He ran as he had never run before, even to catch Yeff. His tail was curled under him. His eyes stung. His nose was blocked with strong wrong smells from the blasts. His head seethed with misery. This was why he had put off coming here. His puppy brain had remembered "Mrs. Canning dear" persuading Mrs. Partridge to have him drowned, but he had not admitted it. To think he had spent long, long ages doting on a being like Duffie! What a flaming green fool! He dashed down concrete paths, past surprised dog faces, past sheds, past an astonished youth with a bucket. The youth dropped the bucket and gave chase too. Sirius sped from him easily. But he felt his Companion coming, quicker than he could run, closer and closer, until she was bringing even to his blocked nose her scent of ozone and jasmine.

There was a house in front of him and its door was open. Sirius shot inside it. His feet skidded helplessly on a polished floor. He fell painfully on his side and slid across a hall, tangling rugs and smashing a gray pot so ugly that it could only have been made by Duffie.

"Yap! What on earth? Yap! Who are you?" A little black poodle, a cosseted house dog, pattered beside him, her nose and eyes bright with curiosity.

"I'm being chased. Is there another door?" said Sirius, heaving himself out of the rugs. His right back leg hurt.

The poodle cocked an ear to the shouts and pounding feet outside. She sniffed the ozone-jasmine smell distastefully. "The other door's down that passage. Shall I hold them up for you?"

"Don't you dare. Keep out of *her* way—the smelly one—whatever you do." Sirius limped across the beastly shiny floor. He could hardly move at human walking pace on it, and his terror increased. He seemed to have bolted into the worst possible place. Behind him, to his surprise, the door of the house crashed shut. The little poodle came skipping gaily after him.

"That's stopped them for a moment. Hurry. They'll come

round the house. This way." She skipped around a corner, where another door stood open on green countryside. "There. Good luck."

"Thank you very much," said Sirius. He ran limping across a stretch of garden and a lane and gathered himself for a gallop across the field beyond. His back leg hurt hideously over the first hundred yards. Then he felt his Companion behind him again. He forgot his leg. He ran. He raced. He crossed the ten-acre field like a hare, except that instinct and fear and green thoughts combined to make him run low and slinking, as the cats did, in order not to make a target for another white sheet of hatred. There was a wood on the skyline. Sirius raced toward it, up a long slope, taking cover in a fold of ground as he went. He tore through a fierce hedge, and climbed another meadow. It was vivid with growing grass. He trod on wrinkled leathery leaves and broke the primroses growing from them with his heavy paws. It seemed a pity, even in his panic. His Companion was closer every step.

As he reached the cool shade of the wood, something held her up. He did not know what it was, but he was sure it would not detain her for very long. He ran up a bank. There was a filthy strong smell there, like a butcher's shop mixed with peppermint. It was coming from a large damp-looking hole. The smell was horrible, but Sirius had no time to be dainty. He squeezed into the hole and pushed his way down it.

It was a tight fit, but it opened out shortly. Sirius, though he had never noticed the fact before, could see in the dark rather better than the cats. He saw that the hole went on beyond the wider part, but he decided to go that way only if he had to. The smelly occupant of the hole was down there somewhere. He turned around, pressing himself against the earthy side of the space, so that, if need be, he could turn around again and face the occupant, and stared anxiously up the way he had come. The entrance to the hole was a dim circle, where grass and leaves fluttered. There was a hint of bright sunlight above and beyond, but it did not strike the mouth of the hole. His Companion seemed to have stopped in the middle of the meadow, about a hundred yards away. He could hear her talking to someone.

". . . not used to being detained in the sphere of my Most Effulgent Consort," she was saying.

"But Effulgency," Sol said, out there, "it is such an unexpected pleasure to find you honoring my humble sphere. I feel I must meet Your Effulgency with proper politeness."

"My dear Sol! There's no need for that!" the Companion answered. "I'm here quite informally."

"But how delightful, Effulgency!" said Sol. His voice dripped golden politeness. "Naturally I should not want to intrude on your privacy, except that, since Your Effulgency is honoring my sphere, I take it that you have come to visit me."

"I don't wish to disappoint you, Sol," began the Companion.

"Effulgency," Sol said, sweetly earnest. "My only disappointment is that you came without my knowledge. That was why I stopped you. I had no wish to be rude, nor to point out that I am of higher effulgence than your honored self, but—"

"Oh, very well," the Companion said crossly. "I'm here on business for my Effulgent Consort, which is secret. Does that satisfy you? Effulgency."

"Effulgency, I must always be satisfied in your presence," Sol said unctuously.

Sirius put his face on his paws and groaned. What a flaming green fool Sol must think he was! It was only too clear Sol knew what his Companion was like. It was equally clear that Sol disliked her intensely. But he had never said a word about her to Sirius. He had always hurried the conversation away from her—no doubt to spare Sirius's feelings. Sirius lay in the damp smelly hole and writhed. He was very grateful to Sol for stopping his Companion, but he could hardly bear to listen to them quarreling so politely.

A voice spoke near his ear. It was a voice as jealously ruffled as Tibbles, the time Sirius turned her off Kathleen's knee. It said, "Who is that being out there? *What* is she?"

There was no new smell, apart from the strong meat-and-peppermint stink and the clay of the walls around him. Sirius supposed it must be the owner of the hole speaking. He dared not offend the creature, whatever it smelled like, so he answered politely, "She's the Companion of Sirius. A white dwarf."

"Then she's a luminary," the voice answered, not at all

pleased. After a stormy pause, it asked, *"Very* beautiful, is she?"

"Very," Sirius answered miserably. And because his Companion was beautiful, he thought, he had made a far worse fool of himself over her than he ever did over Patchie. He had let her lead him as tamely as Kathleen led him on the leash.

"How beautiful?" the voice persisted. "Compare her to something. Is she as beautiful as Sol?"

"Well—" Sirius said helplessly. "They're very different. Yes, I suppose so."

"Then she's more beautiful than the Moon?"

Sirius sighed a little, and wondered why it mattered to this persistent creature. He thought of the living pearly luster of the Companion. He had not seen the Moon often, but he knew it was a dead white in comparison. "Oh yes." He could tell that the creature was not at all pleased to hear this. He tried to explain in terms it would understand. "Put it like this: she's more than the Moon, about the same as Sol, but nothing like as lovely as that meadow with the flowers out there."

"Really!" For some reason, the demanding creature was truly pleased by this. Sirius hoped it would now go away and let him hide with his misery in peace. But it added thoughtfully, "Then, if she's a luminary, I suppose something like a small volcano wouldn't finish her off, would it?"

Sirius did his polite best not to laugh. "I'm afraid not. Luminaries are not like creatures, you know. Sol himself couldn't finish her off without destroying himself too—unless he had a Zoi he could use on her." Then he did not want to talk anymore. He remembered that his Companion had tried to use the Zoi on him. She had knocked him nearly senseless with it while he tried to snatch it away from her.

The demanding creature seemed to be thinking. It did not say anything for a while, and Sirius could hear Sol and his Companion still talking out in the meadow. Sol must have forced the Companion to tell him her business, because she was saying, "I'm sure you have enough to do without looking for Zoi."

"Effulgency," Sol prompted her sweetly.

"Effulgency!" snapped the Companion. "My Consort sent me to find it before it got into the wrong hands."

"But, Effulgency, I must offer my services in my own sphere," Sol replied. "Your Consort would wish it. And that was one of my creatures you tried to kill just now."

"Who cares? Creatures die all the time," said the Companion. She sounded so much like Duffie as she said it that Sirius shivered.

"Effulgency," Sol prompted with dreadful politeness.

"Oh—Effulgency!" said the Companion, cold and furious. "To blazes with you and your creatures! They're not important."

"A correction, Effulgency," said Sol, in melting contempt. "Everything in my sphere is important to me."

The creature in the hole seemed to share Sol's contempt.

Its voice said in Sirius's ear, musingly, "A Zoi could finish her off, you say? Hm."

Sirius knew he ought to get away from this hole. Sol was keeping the Companion talking so that he could. Since the creature in it did not seem unfriendly, he asked it, "Could you help me escape? You see, I'm the creature she tried to kill. That's why I had to come in here without asking you."

"Asking me?" said the voice. "No one asks—" It broke off, and seemed very surprised. "Does that mean you don't know who I am?" That amused it highly. It chuckled, a huge, joyous chuckle that shook the clay walls around Sirius and cheered him as much as it puzzled him. "Then you paid me a real compliment just now, didn't you?"

"Did I?" said Sirius, feeling stupid and confused. "But I've never talked to you before, have I? Er—are you male or female?"

"I've no idea," was the confusing reply. "I've never considered it. And you have talked to me, and I've talked to you—ever since you were a puppy."

"I'm afraid I'm being very stupid," Sirius apologized. He looked carefully around the dim green hole. There was nothing there except the yellow clay walls and the strong smell. He began to think the creature must be invisible. "Is this a silly question too? What do you look like?"

"What you see," said the voice, amused.

"But I can only see—" Sirius suddenly understood. "Earth!" he exclaimed. "How stupid of me! Do forgive me." It was not a creature at all, it was a planet, the most beautiful and kindly he had known. Of course he had talked to Earth. He had done so every time he scoured around the meadow or splashed in the river or sniffed the air. And Earth had talked to him in return, in every living way possible—in scents and sights, in the elegance of Tibbles, the foolish charm of Patchie, in Miss Smith's brusqueness, in Kathleen's kindness, in Basil's roughness and even in Duffie's coldness. Earth contained half the universe and had taught him everything he knew. He did his best to apologize, but Earth was not offended.

"There's no need to keep saying you're sorry. It's Sol's fault. I've listened to him. He deliberately didn't mention me, because you told him you liked me for being green. And I didn't like to speak to you directly, until you were out of Sol's sight. I knew he'd be annoyed."

Sirius thought he did not blame Sol. He knew a number of luminaries who might be tempted to steal Earth if they knew what Earth was like. But he was a little hurt that Sol had not trusted him. Then it struck him that Earth had not been wholly honest with Sol either.

"Look here," he said. "You know where that Zoi is, don't you? Why haven't you told Sol?"

"I'm not going to tell you either," Earth said, and fell into another stormy silence.

Sirius was alarmed. He was afraid he had really offended Earth this time, and just when he needed help most. The meat-and-peppermint smell was stronger, coming in warm gusts along the hole. The real occupant had clearly scented an intruder and was on its way to investigate. Sirius scrambled hurriedly around to face the stink. "I need the Zoi," he said to the earthy wall. "I shall die a dog if I don't have it."

"There are worse fates," said Earth. "Believe me."

"But it's making a mess of your climate," said Sirius.

Earth did not answer. Outside in the meadow, the Companion was losing patience. "Effulgency," she said, high and cold, "if you don't let me go, I shall be forced to damage this wretched planet of yours."

"You just try!" Earth muttered at her.

At that, Sirius remembered how interested Earth had been in what a Zoi might do to the Companion. He saw that Earth was not unwilling to let him find it, if he asked for it in the right way. "Why are you hiding the Zoi?" he asked.

"Because my most unhappy child has it," said Earth. "He hopes it might help him, and so do I. But I can't tell you who he is, because that's against his rules. You know that, too. His hound told you."

The longer hairs of Sirius's back lifted with excitement until they caught on the damp clay. "Yeff, you mean? But he wouldn't say anything."

"He told you the rule," said Earth, and repeated almost exactly what Yeff had said: "No one can ask anything of Yeff's Master unless he has run with his hounds and shared their duties."

When Yeff had said this, it had seemed like nothing. But now Sirius knew Earth was willing to let him find the Zoi but not to tell him where it was, it sounded almost like a promise. "You mean, if I ran with the cold hounds, I might bargain with your child for the Zoi?"

"You might," said Earth. "His rules allow him to bargain."

"Why does he have rules like this?" said Sirius.

"All my darker children have to have strict laws," Earth said. "Sol wouldn't let them exist otherwise."

There seemed such sadness in this that, at any other time, Sirius would have put his nose in his paws and thought about it. But, outside, the Companion's voice was high and angry and Sol's beat against it like the flames in a furnace. Inside the hole, the real occupant was making its way through the last foot or so, snarling shrilly as it came.

"I think you ought to be going now," said Earth.

The animal's pointed snarling face appeared in the hole. It had green eyes too, strong white teeth and reddish fur. It was quite a bit smaller than Sirius, but it was prepared to tear him to pieces all the same.

"What is it?" he asked Earth.

"Get out of here, dog!" snarled the creature. "How dare you sit in my earth!"

"It's a vixen," said Earth. "Vixen, I'm sorry, but I want you to help this dog. Take him through your earth and show him your other entrance."

"I will not!" said the vixen. "I've a litter of cubs back there, and he goes near them over my dead body!"

"And a fat lot of good your dead body will be to your cubs!" said Earth. "Don't be so unreasonable."

"I promise I won't touch your cubs," said Sirius.

"No. You'll come back later with men and spades and more dogs," snapped the vixen. "I know dogs."

"Of course I won't," said Sirius.

"This isn't really a dog," said Earth. "Look at his eyes."

Grudgingly, with her lips drawn back from her teeth, the vixen crouched and stared up at Sirius. "Yes, I see," she said. "But it's not a fox either. What is it?"

"Quite another order of creature from a long way away," Earth told her. "Now let it out through your earth before another creature comes and sets fire to you, him, your cubs and probably the whole wood too."

Stiffly and reluctantly, the vixen turned and crawled back down the hole. "Make haste!" she said to Sirius, flicking the white tip of her brush at him. "I want you out of here."

He squeezed himself after her. It was some distance. The smell was abominable, and grew stronger. Sirius sneezed. He wanted to stand up and stretch, but there was no space. If he had not known that it was Earth all around him, he would have panicked. At length, the vixen crawled out into a lighter, warmer place—a clayey cave, with a hole slanting up from it into bright sunlight. A number of chubby cheerful foxcubs were tumbling about in the sunny patch. Sirius thought they looked rather jolly. He would have liked to stop and play with them. They felt much the same about him. They came bundling playfully toward him, yipping excitedly, obviously under the impression that he was some sort of kindly uncle.

The vixen cuffed them fiercely aside. "Don't go near it!

And," she added to Sirius, "touch a hair of their tails and I'll bite your throat out!"

"I told you I won't hurt them," Sirius protested.

"Maybe. But I can't have them thinking dogs are friendly," the vixen snapped. "A fine mother I'd be if I did! Go up that hole. It comes out on the other side of the wood." As Sirius put his head into the sunlit hole and forced his shoulders after, she added, "There's a stream where you can get a drink down to the right."

After all that running, Sirius was terribly thirsty. "That's thoughtful of you," he called back, as he squeezed his hind legs after his front.

"No it isn't. I just want you gone," snapped the vixen. In her voice he could hear all the strain it was to live in the wild.

12 DRAGGLED, LIMPING and covered with clay, Sirius descended cautiously to the stream and drank. There was no sign of his Companion, but he could not smell clearly. He stank of fox. In order to get rid of the smell, he had to get right into the stream and roll in it. Then he surged out, soaking wet, and limped over plowlands in the direction of home, hoping that Sol would warn him if his Companion came after him again.

Sol said nothing. By the time Sirius reached the town,
he had dried out and looked clean. He hobbled to the yard,
pushed both bolts home, thrust his head into his collar
and crawled into his shelter. It was well he came back
when he did. Duffie remembered him and came out to
make sure he was still there. Sirius gave her a sarcastic
look from under one eyebrow and went to sleep. He was
worn out.

But that night he was wide awake. He sat on Kathleen's
bed, thinking and thinking, until the Moon rose and Tibbles
begged him not to be so restless.

"I can't help it," he said. "Those white dogs with red
ears—you never told me where you saw them."

"Down near the river," said Tibbles. "They've knocked
a lot of houses down there, and it's a good place for field-
mice."

"That place!" said Sirius. "That's always the place! I
wonder if the Zoi fell there—that would explain why it
didn't do any damage."

"What *are* you talking about?" said Tibbles.

"Never mind. When was it? What time of year?"

"I saw them several times. I remember the Moon was
big each time, but I don't remember otherwise."

Sirius bent his head until he had the Moon in view
through the window. It was big now, about a day off full.
He could see a slight flattening at one side. A great sense of
urgency made him get off Kathleen's bed and patter away
downstairs. It was no good. All the doors were locked for
the night. There was no way he could get out to find those

cold hounds and bargain with Earth's unhappy child. There was no way to get out of his dog's body. He was a prisoner twice over—all because he had trusted a cold, white little luminary who had fewer kind feelings even than Duffie.

That was the real thing that was troubling Sirius. He had been such a fool. He roved around the house in his misery, up and down stairs, round and round the living room. The last of his green memories had come out from behind the warm cloud of dog thoughts, and he knew he had not remembered them before because he had not wanted to. They were hateful. His Companion had hated him and tried to get rid of him, and he had not believed it, even when she turned the Zoi on him.

He knew she hated him for not being easy to lead. If she pushed him too far, he got angry. So she had decided to use his rages against him and put the blue luminary from Castor in his place. He was sure the New-Sirius was the same fellow who had been chief witness at his trial. Both he and the Companion had made such a point of the rage Sirius had been in. And he *had* been in a rage. His Companion had first set a little luminary on to annoy him. Then she had taken the Zoi and killed the little luminary in cold blood. Sirius knew she had, although he had no proof. He had simply found her with the corpse and the Zoi. But she had never understood about Zoi, and she had used it so badly that the little luminary's sphere had exploded as he died. Sirius had been furious with her. But he had told himself it was an accident. He had told himself it was an accident even when she aimed the Zoi at him and it had gone hurtling out into Sol's sphere. Then along came the blue luminary while Sirius was half-stunned and said just the soothing sort of things calculated to put anyone in a rage. He had been too angry to think, even when he was arrested—and far, far too trusting. He would not say a word which would incriminate his Companion—but of course every word she had said had made him look more guilty. And he had still not believed she hated him and flown into a rage with the Judges instead. Fool, fool, fool!

"Will you stop tick-tacking about like that!" Remus said. He had managed to avoid being put out that night and was trying for a good night's sleep on a shelf in the kitchen.

"Sorry." Sirius considerately went and sat on the sofa. He rested his chin on the cushions and miserably watched a white line of moonlight move slowly around like a spoke on the floor. He felt as if his green nature had fallen in ruins. He did not think he would ever find that Zoi. The moonlight had moved some way before he remembered Earth saying that there were worse fates than dying a dog. That comforted him. Earth was wise. It was Earth, after all, that had taught him what his Companion was like. Being a dog had its points, and it had certainly saved his life that morning.

He was nearly asleep at last, when his ears pricked and his head lifted. There was something going on in the yard.

"What's that?" Remus asked sleepily, a second or so later.

"Hush!" Sirius was busy listening.

The back door clicked quietly open. Ozone-jasmine

rolled to Sirius's nostrils, and a green scent, achingly familiar except for strange blue overtones, came with it. Sirius slipped silently off the sofa, so that it stood between him and the kitchen door. He was fairly sure his last hour had come. His Companion was back, Sol was around the other side of Earth, and she had brought her Consort, New-Sirius, with her. She had only needed to ask Mrs. Partridge where he lived. Sirius could see the white nimbus from her through the kitchen door, and a blue one overlaid with green from the other.

There was a yowl of terror from Remus. *"There's something strange about these people!"*

After the yowl came a sharp movement, suddenly stopped. "No!" said the Companion. "Leave the creature." It was clear that New-Sirius was well under her thumb. He left Remus alone. Sirius could almost see Remus standing in a stiff arch of terror on the shelf. He wondered what the poor cat made of the speech of luminaries, as the Companion said, "Don't touch any of them except the dog. Sol will bring the whole Galaxy down on us if we give him a chance."

"Blast Sol to blazes!" grumbled New-Sirius. He *was* the chief witness. Sirius recognized his voice. "Who does Sol think he is? He's only a small effulgent."

"Sol," said his Companion, "is a rude, cocksure, bullying, violent, crude little star. In some ways, he reminds me a lot of my late Consort."

"All right, all right," said New-Sirius. "Where is he? This dog?"

"Quite near. Somewhere in there," said the Companion.

The two moved forward. And, as they moved, Remus's nerve broke. He came down from the shelf with the scrambling flop of a cat in real terror and shot wailing away into the distance. Sirius could hear him yowling several backyards off.

That gave Sirius a notion. If he was going to die a dog, at least he should do it properly—just as Remus had behaved like a thoroughly scared cat. He drew a deep breath and began to bark. The noise startled him. He had not realized he had it in him to bay and thunder like this. He braced his four legs and bellowed.

"That's torn it!" said New-Sirius.

"No fire!" the Companion warned him.

They appeared, two black figures, the larger moving in a blue-green aura, the smaller inside a white one. Sirius sensed their two blows coming and darted around the sofa, barking and barking. The sofa shook and sizzled, and lumps came off the back of it. Sirius ran, still barking frantically, for shelter under the dining table. Blows hit the floor behind his back legs, cracking like whips and sparking like electricity. He dived into a forest of wooden legs, chair legs and table legs, and went on barking. A chair flashed and clattered in two under another blow.

"Drive him out. I can't get at him," said New-Sirius.

Sirius crouched, his eyes blazing, baying defiance and anger, and hoping hard. The family was awake. Feet were thumping upstairs. A blow from the Companion cracked on the floor beside him. He had to back away. And *bark,*

bark, bark, squashed against the further chairs.

"What's going on? What have they done to Remus?" Tibbles was on the back of the sofa in a white and spitting arch.

"Get down!" Sirius bayed at her.

He was not sure if she obeyed him or not. New-Sirius, despite a sharp command from his Companion, swung an impatient blow toward the sofa. Blue-green flame smickered. And Tibbles vanished.

Sirius's barking became partly howls of rage and sorrow. The Companion lashed at him again, so that the chairs jumped about. He knew the next blow would force him out on the other side of the table, and New-Sirius was coming around that way to get him.

"Leo! *Leo!* What's happening? Where are you? Oh, *where's* the light?"

Now it was Kathleen. Sirius could see her, dim and white, fumbling at the wall by the door for the light switch. Basil, by the sound, was coming downstairs behind her. But, after what had happened to Tibbles, Sirius knew neither of them was safe. And he was not going to let anyone kill Kathleen. The idea filled him with green rage. He burst out from under the side of the table, scattering one whole chair and the two halves of another, and sprang for the Companion's throat.

He took her completely by surprise. She had not thought he would attack her, and, secretly, she was still very much afraid of him. Instead of striking out, she defended herself.

Kathleen had a momentary and bewildering sight of Leo leaping in a blaze of white light, and then spinning away sideways into the kitchen, snarling. The snarl became a yelp as his side hit the open back door. Then he was out in the yard, barking still, to make sure they went for him, not Kathleen.

They were out in the yard almost as soon as he was. And the yard gate was shut. Sirius had never dreamed he could jump that gate. But, with New-Sirius on his tail, he was in the air before he knew it, with blow after blow striking blue and green just beneath him as he rose. His back legs hit the top of the gate, and he dropped heavily into the lane. He was sure those blows had caught him, and he was almost too winded to stagger away.

"Get up and *run!*" said Earth from underneath him. "Come on!"

He got up. He hobbled. He tried to trot, and the lane was confusingly changed by white slabs of moonlight lying across it. Behind him, the gate clattered and bounced. His enemies, mercifully, were trying to behave like humans. Sirius supposed this was because the Duffields were shouting and switching on lights in the house.

A still, white voice above him said, "Do keep out of my light. I can't stop your coat shining whatever I do. Run in the shadows."

"Thanks, Moon." Sirius veered and hobbled into the black blocks of shadow at the edge of the lane. He saw that it must be the Moon his enemies were trying to deceive.

"Moon, do you know who those are?"

"Sol told me and asked me to keep an eye on you," said the Moon.

"Run!" said Earth. "The gate's open."

At that news, Sirius forgot that his legs hurt. He ran in earnest, low and in the shadows.

"Turn right at the end of the lane," said Earth. "Run like mad for fifty yards. There's a big drain with a stream in it under the road. I'll tell you where."

Sirius raced for the place. His enemies, still acting human, saw which way he turned and pelted after him. The road was empty. So was the crossroad beyond. They came back, flashing cautious blue and white beams into gardens and alleys.

Sirius crouched beneath them in a big round concrete pipe, with his paws in a trickle of water, listening.

"Where is he?" said New-Sirius. "I won't feel safe till he's dead." He sounded both cross and nervous. And no wonder, Sirius thought. He had let the Companion lead him to a point where he could lose both his new sphere and his life. "Suppose he finds the Zoi before we do," he said.

"Quiet," said the Companion. "I don't think this planet is a fool, nor its satellite either."

"They can't do anything," muttered New-Sirius. "Just wait till I find that Zoi. Then they'll have to keep quiet, or the whole system will have an accident." He stopped. Somewhere near a car was coming, fast. "What's that?"

"It may be their police," said the Companion. "We'd

better hide. We can catch the dog easily when he tries to get home."

Sirius listened to them receding. "Where are they?" he asked Earth.

"I've lost them," said Earth. "Just a moment." There was a busy pause. Sirius drank from the trickle of water and waited. The car stopped, somewhere near. "The Moon thinks they're hiding behind the chimneys on the roof of your house," Earth reported. "The police have just got there. Go out through the other end of this pipe and you won't be seen. Don't try to go home till Sol can see you."

"Thank you," Sirius said gratefully.

He crawled out of the pipe a street away and set off at once toward the center of the town. He crossed empty roads. He passed the silent Town Hall and trotted by lit-up deserted shops, growing sadder and sadder as he went. He knew he dared not go home at all now. Sol could protect him by day, but at night his enemies would come for him. In a way, it made things easier. He could hide in the place where the houses had been knocked down, and his providers would feed him. If he watched that place long enough, he was sure he would find the cold hounds, and the Zoi. He would just have to hope his enemies did not find him first. But he wished he did not feel so lonely and so sad.

He trotted mournfully into the cindery stretch, past the quiet, hooded bulldozers. Rank, wet smells came from the overgrown part. He was trotting toward them, when large paws beat on the cinders behind him. Sirius whirled around, bristling. For a moment, he thought it was Yeff. The coat shone like frost under the Moon, and the dog's ears seemed to be red.

"It's all right. It's only me. What luck meeting you!" said Bruce.

Sirius was overjoyed. He was not alone anymore. He bounded forward, wagging his tail, and Bruce ran to meet him. They stood nose to nose, tails softly waving, absolutely delighted.

"You see? I did get out," Bruce said. "I pulled the whole wretched lock off this morning just after you left. I looked for you. You do get about, don't you? I followed your scent all over town. I've never had such fun in my life. I met three old men, one after another, who all thought I was you and gave me things to eat. Then I went to an old lady's house, and she knew I wasn't you. She told me to go home, but she gave me a bone first. Then two policemen tried to catch me, and I had to pretend I was playing with them in order to get away. I can't tell you all the things that happened! But I was getting awfully lonely when you came along. To tell the truth, I'd just decided to go home."

"Would you mind staying out for a while?" Sirius asked. "I'd be glad of company. Things have gone rather badly for me tonight."

"Not at all!" said Bruce. "I meant to stay out as long as I could. I'll show you the place I found to sleep in, shall I?"

They trotted side by side into the grass and weeds. Bruce

went to a mound of rubble near the middle. It had been there so long that bushes and small trees had sprung up on it. On the darker side of it was a thicket of elders growing around a dry and sheltered hollow. Bruce pushed his way into it, through the husky, juicy smell of new elder leaves.

"Not bad, eh?" he said.

"Perfect," said Sirius.

They settled down and curled up, with their warm, heavy backs pressed against one another, wheezing little grunts because it was so good to have company. Then, dog fashion, they fell straight into a deep sleep.

A couple of hours later, they both jerked awake, pricked their ears, and had almost pushed their way out through the trees before Bruce became rational.

"We can't," he said. "It's not meant for us."

The sound which had wakened them came again—haunting, imperious, and very loud and near. Though they knew it was not calling to them, they both surged forward through the whippy trees. The Moon was low, almost behind the houses, and yellowish. On the other side of the sky, Sol's coming was marked by a white stain. And in front of the mound, across the cleared space, dogs were streaming. They came in a helter-skelter confusion of glittering white coats and cat-like yellow eyes. The only sound they made was the frosty patter of paws. Like cats, they ran silent. The loud blasts of that imperious horn were soundless ones. Yet, in spite of their silence, that madly running crowd of dogs was utter wildness—wilder than the vixen snarling in her earth—something so wild it was wrong and strange and confused.

Sirius took one look and dashed to join the racing dogs.

They were running at an angle to him. As he bounded across the rubbly ground, the foremost dogs were already disappearing. With every step Sirius took, the number of dogs he was trying to catch got fewer and fewer. And, just as he caught up with the last dog, it was gone too. It was as if it had run behind an invisible wall. Sirius overran the spot, and there was nothing beyond. After that point there was not even the frosty scent of the dog.

Furiously disappointed, he ran around in a circle. The scent simply stopped where the dog had vanished. The weeds and rubble were exactly the same on both sides of the place. But the dogs were simply not there. "Earth," he said. "Please, Earth, where have they gone?"

"I'm sorry," Earth answered. "It's not my secret."

Sirius flung up his head and looked at the Moon. "Moon, how often do they run? Please tell me."

The Moon was almost behind the houses, and the answer was a little muffled. "Yesterday, today and tomorrow when I'm full. Then not for a month."

"Thank you," said Sirius. "Thank you for all your help."

"It was nothing," said the Moon. "Sol told me to help you."

"And I told you to keep your mouth shut as you usually do!" Earth said.

"You said to give him all the help I could, tonight," the Moon said, injured but smug, and sank out of sight behind the roofs. Not that this stopped the argument. Sirius could hear Earth's voice pursuing the Moon, right to the horizon. But he was busy sniffing the ground, now blue-gray with the signs of Sol's coming. Here was another strange thing. Every trace of the frosty scent of those dogs had vanished the moment the Moon went.

Bruce joined him, looking nervous and puzzled. "They didn't leave a scent. Why is that? What are they?"

"Something very peculiar," said Sirius. "And I *have* to run with them tomorrow, if it kills me!"

"That might be rather fun," said Bruce. "You could get away with it easily. Apart from your collar, you look exactly like them by moonlight."

"So do you," said Sirius. "Didn't you know?"

"Then I'll come too!" Bruce said gleefully.

"Really? That will make two nights you'll be away from home," Sirius said. "What about your people?"

Bruce became rather thoughtful. "Oh well—I'll go back first thing the next morning," he said. "But I must do this first. I've never had such an adventure. The only thing is— my master works near here during the day and I don't want to be tempted. Can you think of anywhere else we could go?"

Sirius thought. After the day and the night he had had, he longed to spend the next twelve hours safely curled up in a nice warm sofa. Who—? "I wonder," he said. "If we went to Miss Smith and looked really pleading, she might let us stay in her house for today. She's the old lady who knew you weren't me."

"Oh, I liked her!" said Bruce. "Let's go!"

They set off at a swift busy trot. The street lights looked pale. Some houses already had lights on inside, and there were a number of cars about. Several times Sirius had to implore Bruce to be careful. Bruce was not good at roads.

When they were more than halfway to Miss Smith's house, Sol came up behind them with a shout. "What's this Earth tells me?"

He sounded so annoyed that Sirius ran rather faster, not at all sure he wanted to face him. "I—er—I talked to Earth. I'm sorry if you don't like it."

"Not that!" blazed Sol. "Your Companion and her Consort. Did they really dare?"

"Yes," said Sirius. "But I'm all right, thanks to Earth." He glanced back at Sol and grinned.

Sol was white with wrath. "If they harm a hair of your coat, I'll ruin them!" he said. "I warned her! I can't lawfully stop them prowling about, but you are *de facto* one of my creatures, and they mustn't touch you. I'm glad you got away. It was a clever idea to have one of your brothers with you. That should confuse her."

"It wasn't meant like that," Sirius answered, rather alarmed. "I don't want Bruce hurt."

"You should have the other three, too," said Sol. "They wouldn't dare hurt any of you until they knew which was you." He did not say anything more for a second. Sirius thought he had turned his attention elsewhere. He was surprised when Sol said suddenly, "What do you think of Earth?"

"What a question!" said Sirius. "You know Earth's a masterpiece."

He could feel Sol beaming on his back, as pleased as Earth had been the day before. "Mars isn't bad," Sol said, defensively.

Sirius laughed. He was so taken up with his amusement that he did not notice a police car gliding to the curb beside him. Its doors opened and policemen leaped out.

"Run!" woofed Bruce, and was off up the pavement like the wild hunt.

Sirius was taken by surprise. He started after Bruce, and was brought up short by a policeman's hand in his collar. He ducked and wriggled and almost slipped out of the collar. The policeman seized him by the scruff of his neck instead.

"Come on, my lad. In that car."

Sirius struggled, but the policeman won. Sirius was bundled onto a sort of leather plowed field, which seemed to be the back seat of the car, while, at the end of the street, the other two policemen gave up chasing Bruce and came panting back.

"There *were* two!" one of them puffed. "I couldn't believe it when those descriptions came in. Which one have we got?"

The policeman holding Sirius looked at the disk on his collar. "I thought so! My old friend Leo! Cheer up, Leo. You're a hero today. Makes a change from last time."

13

FEELING RATHER sick from the swift, swirling ride, Sirius was delivered at the Duffields' house. Kathleen ran at him and hugged him. "Oh, Leo!" Robin pounced on him from the other side. "Shamus, you *are* brave!" Basil tweaked his tail. "You silly old Rat! What did you get lost for?" Even Mr. Duffield patted his head and called him a good horse. Duffie sniffed. "Sentimental idiots! What are dogs for, if not to keep off burglars?"

Sirius discovered, to his acute embarrassment, that he was supposed to have saved the house from burglars. The burglars were supposed to have been armed. New-Sirius had not been careful. Perhaps he could not be. Sirius knew that it was not easy for a high effulgent to use force without heat. At any rate, all the Duffields had seen the yard full of vivid green flashes as he struck at Sirius. Some of them had burned grooves in the gate. Indoors, the broken chair had been smoldering. And there was the queer wound on Tibbles.

Tibbles was sitting in a basket lined with a blanket, and the electric heater was on specially for her. Sirius ran to her delightedly. Tibbles put a rather shaky nose up to greet him. She looked ill. "Hallo," she said. "I thought you were dead."

"I thought you were, too. What happened?"

"I think I *would* have been dead if you hadn't shouted

at me," Tibbles said. "I was in the middle of jumping down off the sofa when he hit me, and the sofa got most of it."

Sirius looked at the sofa. There were large lumps out of its back, from which greenish fluff and horsehair were oozing. He looked at Tibbles's back. There was a raw, slanting weal on her. The fur around it was singed green. "Shall I lick it better?" he asked.

"It hurts when it's touched," she said. "It's a wrong kind of hurt. I don't think those were real people."

"They weren't," he said. "That's why I may be able to lick it better for you."

"Try," she said.

Sirius waited for a moment, while he tried to draw on any virtue there might be left in his green nature. He was not sure he had any. But he knew he now had as much of his green nature as could be crammed into a dog, and he was sure that only that could heal Tibbles. Then he bent and licked the weal.

Kathleen hurried to stop him. "No, Leo. Leave!"

"Let him," said Mr. Duffield. "Animals know what they're doing."

"Romulus and Remus wouldn't touch it, though," Basil objected.

Tibbles winced at the first lick, but, after the third, she began to purr. "Oh that's better! It's gone cool. Go on."

Duffie threw herself on the battered sofa and announced that she was worn out. "I suppose we'd better have breakfast," she said. Kathleen, who looked quite as tired, hurried away to the kitchen. It seemed that the whole family had been up ever since Sirius woke them by barking. They had spent the rest of the night explaining things to the police, describing their dog, trying to describe two burglars no one had clearly seen, hunting around the house to see what had been stolen, wondering about the peculiar damage and nursing Tibbles.

When Kathleen had breakfast ready, Mr. Duffield switched the radio on for the early news and remarked that the horse should have some cornflakes, too, as a reward. So Kathleen put down a snickering golden plateful. Sirius loved cornflakes. He left Tibbles purring sleepily, with her back the proper color again, and attacked the plateful in sloshy gollops. Through the noise he was making, he suddenly gathered that something strange had happened. The whole family was leaning toward the radio, looking tense and surprised.

"Isn't that the prison where your father is?" Robin said.

"I think one of them's him," Kathleen answered in a queer, subdued voice. Sirius could not tell if she was very sad or very happy. He did his best to follow for once the flat monotonous voice from the radio.

"Two of the escaped men," he heard, "were recaptured by the army in the early hours of this morning. O'Brien, the third man, is still at large." The radio went on to talk of other things, leaving Kathleen looking so excited, joyful and frightened that Sirius wished he had heard more. He went pensively back to his cornflakes, remembering that letter Kathleen's father had sent her a month before. Perhaps Kathleen's father had not meant he was going to be released. Perhaps the letter was so crumpled and dirty because it had been smuggled out to warn Kathleen he was going to escape. He could see Kathleen thought so.

She was not the only one. As soon as Mr. Duffield had gone upstairs to shave, Duffie rounded on Kathleen. "I warn you, Kathleen, I don't intend to help that father of yours to break the law. I never wanted to get mixed up with convicts. I told Harry I wasn't having you. I knew how it would be. And I was right. If that man tries to come here, I shall have him back in jail again before he can say knife. You can tell him I said so."

It was doubtful if Kathleen heard her. She was in a daze of happiness and anxiety. "I *know* it's my Daddy they haven't caught!" she whispered as she was tying Sirius up in the yard as usual. "I do hope he gets away. He's awfully clever, so maybe he will."

Sirius sat half inside his shelter and pondered about it. He decided he was glad. Kathleen's father could not have escaped at a better time. That night, Sirius himself would have to leave. Whether he found the Zoi or not, he would not dare to go on living here now. But, now he came to think about it, he was sad and uneasy at the thought of leaving Kathleen alone. It was not kind. So it made a great deal of difference that her father had escaped. He could look after Kathleen in the future. Sirius was quite aware that Ireland was some way away, over some water, and that the police did not allow people to remain escaped from prison. But he comforted his slightly uneasy conscience by telling himself that Kathleen had said her father was very clever. No doubt he would manage to come and fetch Kathleen somehow. Then Kathleen would be happy again.

"Don't think you're going to jump that gate again while I'm here!" Duffie said, stumping out into the yard to make sure Sirius was there. Lack of sleep had made her restless, and more than usually bad-tempered. She stumped into the yard six times that morning.

Each time, Sirius gave her that sarcastic look from under one eyebrow. He knew it annoyed her. He had no intention of leaving yet. The time to go was when everyone would least expect it, just before Kathleen was due home from school. But it was a pity, Sirius thought, settling down to sleep, that he would not be able to say good-by to Kathleen properly.

About midday, Sol flicked a beam of light over his muzzle and woke him up. "Were you intending to go somewhere else tonight?" Sol asked.

Sirius opened one eye. "Yes. To find the Zoi if possible."

"Then I'd better warn you," said Sol, "that you may want to change your mind. I wish I knew how to advise you. Things are going to be very difficult now."

"What are you talking about?" said Sirius, opening both eyes.

Sol did not answer. He simply spilled a bright golden wedge of light on the back door. Kathleen came out into it. Sirius sprang to his feet in amazement. He had never known Kathleen to come home at this hour before. His tail wagged madly. He was delighted. Now he could say good-by as he should.

Kathleen crossed the yard in an odd blundering way, as if she could not see where she was going very well. A strange lady came out after her and watched Kathleen anxiously. She seemed worried about her. Sirius saw Kathleen's face was a yellowish white, almost the color of his coat. Something was the matter with her. Kathleen put out her hands in a vague fumbling way to untie the rope, and Sirius stood on his hind legs with his paws on her arm and tried to see what was wrong.

Kathleen said, in a peculiar, flat voice, "This is Leo, Miss Markles. I told you he would look after me." ¯

"He looks a beautiful dog, dear," Miss Markles said. Sirius knew she was nervous of him and kindly trying to hide it from Kathleen. "Why don't you bring him indoors with you, dear?"

She led the way back through the kitchen. Kathleen followed, keeping her hand tight on Sirius's collar, and sat listlessly down on the battered sofa. Very puzzled and worried, Sirius hopped up beside her and sat watching her pale, stiff face.

"Now, dear," said Miss Markles, still trying hard to be kind, "can I get you a cup of tea?"

"No, thank you," Kathleen said flatly. "I'm quite all right. I've got Leo."

"Well, in that case—" Miss Markles said, dubiously hovering. She seemed to give Kathleen up. It was an obvious relief to her. "Then if you think you'll be all right with Leo, dear, I'd better go and have a word with Mrs. Duffield."

Kathleen did not answer. Miss Markles, giving her a

nervous look, went and tapped timidly on the door to the shop. Nobody answered the tap, but she nevertheless opened the door, tiptoed through, and closed it again so softly that Sirius hardly heard the latch click.

"She's the school secretary," Kathleen explained to him, in that odd, dull voice, staring stiffly in front of her. "She's doing her best to be kind, but I don't think she's had much practice. They've all been like that, ever since—" She put out an arm and clutched Sirius against her. After three minutes, Sirius had to wriggle. His back was twisted. He nosed her face apologetically and squirmed into a more comfortable position. Kathleen leaned her head on him. "Oh, Leo," she said. "My Daddy's dead. The police got Uncle Harry out of work and they came round to school. The other side found him before the army did. They shot him dead this morning. And, Leo, the worst of it is, I can't remember what my Daddy *looked* like properly—not after all this time. I keep trying to remember, and it gets in the way of being sad."

Sirius nosed her again, truly sorry. He saw what Sol had meant. He had no idea what to do now.

"I'd no idea what a muddle being sad is," Kathleen said. She sounded much more like her usual self, saying it. Sirius was glad. "I almost keep forgetting my Daddy's dead. And then I wonder if it hurt, and hope it didn't, and I hope he wasn't horribly frightened. Then, in the middle, I remember how annoying he could be sometimes. He was quite like Uncle Harry. If he didn't like something, he didn't want to know about it. But he was funny and kind, too. And I know all that, but I can't remember what he *looked* like." Still hugging Sirius, she went back to staring straight ahead again. He wondered if he should nose her. Or not. He did not know what to do.

The door to the shop burst open. Duffie trampled in, high and cold and furious.

"What on earth does that woman mean, bringing you back here in the middle of the day?" she demanded. "I pay a small fortune for you to have school lunches. Am I supposed to pay for it twice today, or what?"

"It's all right," Kathleen said, still staring at nothing. "I'm not hungry."

But Duffie had only said that to warm herself up for her real diatribe. "Then starve if you'd rather," she said. "I know by now you do everything just to annoy me. *You* don't care! Look at you, sitting there with that great useless dog messing up the sofa, with not an ounce of consideration for *me!* And, to crown it all, that woman tells me to comfort you! Let me tell you, Kathleen, it should be the other way round. I've put up with you for nearly a year, and you've been nothing but trouble and expense the whole time. I only agreed to have you on the understanding that you'd go back to that father of yours as soon as he came out of jail. Now look what happens! He gets himself shot, and I have to put up with you for the rest of your life! Harry'll be trying to make me adopt you next. Well, that's one thing I *won't* do. I told that woman to her face I wouldn't. The wretched child can go to a Home, I told her. As for the father, he only got exactly what he deserved!"

"He didn't deserve to be shot," Kathleen said drearily. "Nobody does—even you."

"I'm not going to stand here and be insulted!" said Duffie. "Since they thought fit to send you home at this unreasonable hour, you can make yourself useful for once. Go and turn out Robin's room. It's a pigsty. You've not touched it for weeks."

"No," said Kathleen, without interest. "Do it yourself if you want it done."

"Don't you take that tone with me!" Duffie said. It did not seem to occur to her that a great calamity had just fallen on Kathleen, nor that even Kathleen could be pushed too far. "I've taken you in. I've lavished kindness on you. Do as I tell you."

Kathleen stood up. Sirius could feel her trembling. "No," she said. "You've never been kind to me, not for a minute. Why should I do your dirty work?"

Duffie stared at her, coldly outraged. Kathleen was standing so still, apart from the trembling, and she spoke in such a dead, calm voice, that Duffie still did not see she had gone too far. She said, "I've had about enough of you, Kathleen!"

Kathleen said quietly, "And I've had about enough of you." Very slowly and deliberately, though she was still shaking, she walked to the broom cupboard and took out a broom. Sirius ran anxiously after her along the sofa, wondering what she was going to do.

"Take that broom upstairs and get to work," said Duffie. "I'm going to get myself some lunch." She aimed a slap at

Sirius as she tramped off to the kitchen. "Get down, you filthy creature!"

The slap did not hurt much, but two pink places appeared on Kathleen's face, under her eyes, making her eyes look dark as the night sky. She looked as if she had come alive again. "Don't you hit Leo!" she shouted at Duffie's back. "I'll show you!" And she dashed into the shop waving the broom.

"What's she doing?" Tibbles asked anxiously from her basket.

A great crashing of pots was the answer. Sirius arrived in time to see Kathleen put the broom to the second shelf of pottery and sweep sideways. Pots rained down, pots by tens, twenties and thirties, smashing, crashing, smashing. Bits flew across the floor. Dust rose. Sirius jumped, wincing, among them and tried to nose Kathleen to bring her to her senses.

Kathleen's broom swept along another shelf, and another. Her hair was wild and her face bright red. *"Hurray!"* she shouted, above the crashing. "I've always wanted to do this!" With Sirius still dancing uneasily about her, she jumped on a pile of pieces. Sharp bits flew. She raised the broom and brought it down on a stack of pots by the salesroom door. *Smash! Parangrash! Crunch!* She jumped on them. By this time, there was not a whole pot in the workroom. Kathleen whirled her broom and rushed toward the shop itself.

Duffie pounded in and caught her in its doorway. There

was a brief, fierce struggle. Then Duffie was hitting Kathleen with the broom, with both bulging calves braced to hold her, and Kathleen was screaming. Sirius did not think. As soon as Kathleen screamed, his teeth went into Duffie's left calf, almost of their own accord. He brought his jaws together vehemently.

Duffie yelled. She tasted horrible. Sirius let go, disgusted, and leaped away, not quite in time. The broom caught him across the head, and he yelped. He dodged. Duffie hopped furiously about after him, crushing shards of pot under her right sandal, aiming swipes at him with the broom and raving.

"That does it! That's final! The filthy brute! I shall die of blood poisoning!"

"You've probably poisoned him," Kathleen said.

Duffie leaned on the broom like a crutch and tried to see her leg. "I'm bleeding like a pig!"

"No you're not," Kathleen said scornfully. "It's only a trickle. He could have bitten a piece out if he'd wanted."

"He's not going to have the chance again!" raved Duffie. "As soon as I've put a Band-Aid on, he's going down to the vet's. And as for you, you're going to pay for every single pot!"

"All right," said Kathleen. "But you're not taking Leo to be put down."

"Oh, yes I am!" said Duffie. "This very afternoon. We're none of us safe from the brute!"

Kathleen turned away and walked over the scattered pottery to the door. "Come on, Leo. Mind your feet." Sirius picked his way after her, trembling. He could tell Duffie meant what she said. He hoped Kathleen would put him in the yard, so that he would have a chance to escape.

"Where are you going?" Duffie screeched, hobbling after them.

"I'm taking him down to the vet myself," said Kathleen. "You're not doing it." She went to the broom closet and fetched the leash. "Here, Leo."

Sirius stood in the middle of the living room, appalled. He supposed Kathleen had little choice, but he still could not believe she could do it. Kathleen called to him sharply. He did not go to her. Kathleen went to him and grabbed his collar, unusually roughly, while she wrestled to get the leash clipped on. Sirius only let her do it in the end because he knew he could slip out of the collar.

"Now, come on!" Kathleen said peremptorily and lugged him to the side door.

"He'll be closed for lunch," Duffie said, limping to the kitchen for a Band-Aid.

"I'll wait outside till he opens," said Kathleen, and shut the door with a slam. Sirius could still hardly believe it. His back bristled, his tail was low, and he refused to move. Kathleen backed up the passage, heaving at him. "Don't be an idiot!" she snapped. "Come *on!*" A truck passed in the road beyond. Under the noise of it, Kathleen leaned down and whispered, "Of course we're not going to the vet, you idiot! But she wouldn't have let us out of the house if I hadn't said it. Now, do come on."

Hugely relieved, Sirius surged forward. By the time they

reached the end of the street, it was he who was pulling and Kathleen who was hanging back. He look around to see why. Tears were rolling down her face.

"I don't know where to go, Leo," she said. "I've just noticed there isn't anywhere. If I go and tell Uncle Harry, he'll only take us back. Then she'll have you put down. I don't know what to do."

It was certainly a problem. Sirius tugged Kathleen on again and thought about it. He owed it to Kathleen to make sure she was safe before he left her to hunt for the Zoi. She had looked after him. He must do the same for her. But where could he take her? A little doubtfully, he thought of Miss Smith. He liked Miss Smith. He was sure she would like Kathleen. But he knew that people would take in a dog far more readily than they would take in a fellow human. It was odd, but it was true. Still, he could think of nobody more likely than Miss Smith, and he found he had set off unconsciously dragging Kathleen toward Miss Smith's house anyway. He began to drag her faster. Kathleen's feet hurried and stumbled behind.

"Where are we going, Leo? The Town Hall? But we can't just go and complain to the Mayor, can we? Would he listen?"

The idea appealed to Kathleen. Before long, she had it so firmly in her head that they were going to the Town Hall to complain to the Mayor, that Sirius had great difficulty in leading her any other way. As they got near Miss Smith's house, he had to prod and push her at every corner.

"Where are you going? This isn't the way," she kept saying.

In the end, Sirius put his shoulders forward, braced his hind legs and heaved Kathleen bodily up the street where Miss Smith lived. He heaved her past the stack of dustbins and up the steps to Miss Smith's front door. He put out a paw to the mark he had made knocking on it every day, and just managed to batter on it while Kathleen was pulling him down the steps again. The door opened almost at once.

"Oh, now the lady's coming!" Kathleen said, horribly embarrassed. "Really, Leo!"

"Do you call him Leo?" said Miss Smith. "I call him Sirius, because of his eyes. Hallo, Sirius. So you've brought your mistress now, have you?"

"I'm awfully sorry. He pulled me here," Kathleen explained.

Miss Smith looked up from Sirius to her stiff, tear-marked face. "Would you like to come in and perhaps have a cup of tea while you tell me what's happened?" she suggested.

"Well, I—" Kathleen began. Sirius heaved again and they went up the steps and in through the door in a rush.

"That's right," said Miss Smith, shutting the front door behind them. "Now, tea and bones."

At this moment, Bruce, who, like Sirius, was not much given to barking, cautiously put his face around Miss Smith's sitting-room door to see who was there. Sirius had forgotten Bruce would be here. He heaved Kathleen forward again to greet him. "She let you stay? I *am* glad to see you!"

"You've got a dog just like Leo!" said Kathleen.

Miss Smith looked a trifle guilty. "Actually, he's not mine at all. His collar says he's called Bruce, and he seems to come from those houses down by the river. He turned up this morning before I was up and begged me to let him stay. I suppose he has his reasons. I think he's a friend of your Leo's."

"He must be," Kathleen agreed, watching the waving tails of both dogs.

Before long, they were all four in Miss Smith's sitting room, Bruce and Sirius with a bone apiece, and Kathleen with a strong sugary cup of tea.

"Now," said Miss Smith, "what did your Leo do? Or was it both of you?"

Kathleen began to cry. "Both of us. I took a broom and smashed all Mrs. Duffield's pots—"

"Mrs. Duffield's pots?" said Miss Smith. "You mean that awful little shop in Mead Bank? Then I congratulate you. Those are quite the most hideous things in town. There ought to be a law against them. Then what?"

"Duffie hit me with the broom and Leo bit her," Kathleen said despairingly.

"Good dog!" said Miss Smith. She bent down and patted Sirius so heartily that his ribs boomed and he all but swallowed his bone whole. "A dog's not much good if he doesn't look after you," she told Kathleen.

"Yes, but Duffie was going to have him put down," said

Kathleen. "So we had to run away."

"I see," said Miss Smith. "But you've left an awful lot out, my dear. Neither you nor Sirius are the kind of people who break pots or bite people without good reason."

"No," said Kathleen. "I mean, I've always wanted to break them, because I think they're ugly too, and I'm sure Leo must have wanted to bite Duffie all his life, only—" She took a deep gulping breath and began to talk very fast. The teacup shook between her hands and tears rolled into it, until Miss Smith took it firmly away. She told Miss Smith her father had been shot, and what Duffie had said. Then she went on to all the things she had not been able even to tell Leo. "I can't *say* things while they're happening," she confessed. "It just makes them worse." She told Miss Smith how homesick and miserable she had been when she came to live with the Duffields, and how lonely, and how none of them liked her except Robin, and how Duffie did not want her and complained at spending money on her.

She went too fast for Bruce. He only understood one thing, and that shocked him. "Did you really bite someone?" he asked Sirius.

"Yes," said Sirius, "for being horrible to Kathleen. Wouldn't you have done? What would you do if someone started hitting your master?"

"It would worry me awfully," said Bruce. "But everyone likes my master, so I don't think it would happen."

"Everyone ought to like Kathleen too," said Sirius. "She's been unlucky."

Miss Smith seemed to agree. She shook her head repeatedly while Kathleen told her how angry Duffie had been when she brought home the nearly drowned puppy, and how she had agreed to do all the housework if Duffie would let her keep Leo instead of a birthday present. "And she's always hated him," Kathleen said. "But I suppose it was fair, because dogs do make a mess. But she scolds me and scolds me. And I don't always remember things, and then she says she'll have Leo put down. And I dried the turkey out at Christmas, because I'd never cooked one before. Then Leo got fleas and I had to spring-clean. It was awful hard work, and when I got back to school I was so tired I couldn't *think,* and of course a lot of the boys said that was because I was Irish and didn't have a brain. And they chased me every day and called names, until Leo frightened them off. Only that was no good because they complained to the police and said Leo was a savage creature, and Duffie said I'd let him out on purpose."

"This doesn't sound fair to me at all," said Miss Smith. "Is there a Mr. Duffield? What does he think?"

"Yes, he's quite kind," said Kathleen. "But he doesn't notice unless something makes him uncomfortable."

"I see," said Miss Smith.

Kathleen was suddenly conscience-stricken. "I shouldn't be complaining to you, Miss Smith. It's nothing to do with you. I'm a perfect stranger."

"Nonsense!" said Miss Smith. "It was clever of Sirius to bring you. I wish he'd brought you before. Now, we must see what's to be done." She thought for a while. There was no sound except the loud ticking of the clock that would only work on its face and the crunching as Bruce finished his bone. Kathleen took an uneasy look at Miss Smith's stern old face. Then she picked up her cup and pretended to be drinking cold tea.

"The real difficulty," Miss Smith said abruptly, "is your Leo. Somebody has complained about him before, you see. Not that I blame him. Luckily, I used to teach the Mayor, and Inspector Plum, and that Superintendent Higg— naughty child, he used to be—so something might be done. But you're a much simpler case, Kathleen. We mustn't let you stay with the Duffields a moment longer. I'd better see about that at once, before this Mrs. Duffield starts complaining to people about her pots. You'll stay quietly here with me for now—"

"Oh, I can't do that!" Kathleen said.

"Yes, you can," Miss Smith said fiercely. "I've been very lonely since my Lass died, and I've not felt much use to anyone since I retired. I shall be glad to have you. And what I was going to say was, if we find we get on—and we may not, because I am a highly independent and crotchety person, you'll find, Kathleen—then perhaps you might like to stay here for good. Would you like to give it a trial?"

Kathleen put down the cold tea and seemed about to cry again. "Oh, I can't really? And Leo?"

"And Leo, of course," said Miss Smith.

14

INSTEAD OF RESTING that afternoon, Miss Smith wrote letters, while Kathleen took a nap on Miss Smith's spare bed. It seemed to Sirius, staring at Miss Smith's racing pen and the growing pile of envelopes, that Miss Smith had at one time taught everyone of importance in the town, from the Member of Parliament to the man in charge of the R.S.P.C.A. Sirius thought she was rather enjoying herself. When Kathleen came downstairs, she was much more cheerful. She enjoyed herself washing Miss Smith's kitchen floor, and then got tea, with scones, in Miss Smith's gold-edged tea set.

"I didn't ask you here to do *my* housework!" Miss Smith kept snapping crossly as she wrote.

"But I like to, because you're such a dear," Kathleen called back.

Sirius and Bruce left large pawprints on the wet floor going out through the dog-door into the garden. They settled that they would leave as soon as Miss Smith and Kathleen went to bed. Then, somehow, they found themselves romping like puppies, up and down the grass and over the tangled flowerbeds, struggling furiously for possession of a ribbed stocking that must have belonged to Miss Smith. When the stocking came to pieces, they went indoors and ate buttered scones. After that they lay snoozing, while Miss Smith finished her letters and Kathleen curled up with one of Miss Smith's many books.

When Miss Smith had posted her letters, and only then, she telephoned the Duffields. Sirius bristled. He could hear Duffie at the other end. "Kathleen and her dog are with me," Miss Smith said. "My name is Smith." Then, after a pause filled with cold, strident talk from the telephone, she said, "My good woman, complain to whom you please. I don't intend to listen to a word of it." She slammed the receiver down and came back to her chair, looking militant.

"You didn't say your address," Kathleen said.

Miss Smith chuckled. "That's the best of being called Smith. It will take them some days to find out *which* Smith. I don't want the woman bothering us until we've got something settled."

Nevertheless, halfway through the most peaceful evening Sirius had ever spent, the telephone jangled. When Miss Smith answered it, Sirius found his ears pricking up at the high voice inside it. "I've no idea what you're talking about," said Miss Smith. "Who is Shamus?" The high voice corrected itself. "Or Leo," said Miss Smith. "A dog? Goodness me, I'm not a pet shop!" She put the receiver down. "One of your Duffields seems to be trying to find you," she said to Kathleen. "He sounded very young."

"Robin!" Kathleen exclaimed. "Oh dear, I hadn't thought! Robin must be missing us terribly."

"He's welcome to visit you as soon as we've sorted things out," said Miss Smith.

After all those letters, Miss Smith was tired. She went to bed early, telling Kathleen to remember to lock the door and switch the lights out when she had finished her book. Kathleen had seemed to be absorbed in her book. But, as soon as Miss Smith was upstairs, she laid it quietly aside and sat staring in front of her. After a while, tears began to trickle down her face.

"And I shouldn't have broken Duffie's pots," she told Sirius, out of her misery. "That was because my Daddy was shot. It wasn't what Duffie said at all. I told you what a muddle being sad is."

Sirius came and sat on her feet, leaning against her to comfort her. Kathleen twisted her fingers in his collar gratefully, but she went on crying. After an hour, Sirius became anxious. It was not long now to moonrise. He had found Kathleen a home and a friend. But she plainly still needed him too. He wondered if he would be able to leave at all.

Bruce became frankly impatient. He got up and wandered around the room. He nosed the door open and looked meaningly at Sirius.

"You go," Sirius said. "I'll meet you by our elder trees if I can get away."

"Really?" said Bruce. "I don't want to miss that hunt, but—"

"Go on," said Sirius. "You can do me a favor, if I don't come. When the hunt's over, ask the Master of it for a thing called a Zoi. If he gives it to you, bring it to me."

"A Zoi," said Bruce. "All right. I'll see you."

He tick-tacked quietly away through the hall and the kitchen. The dog-door thumped. Kathleen took no notice. She just sat there with her hand twisted in Sirius's collar and cried. Another worry came to Sirius. His Companion must be looking for him. The later it grew, the more certain it was that she had found out he was not at the Duffields'. She would search the town, and he would be forced to go on his own to the cleared space while she searched. She could easily find him, and Earth might not be able to help him this time.

Bruce had been gone nearly an hour, when Miss Smith's doorbell rang.

Kathleen jumped. "Oh, Leo, suppose it's Duffie! Should I answer it?"

Sirius got up and went quietly to the front door. He sniffed cautiously at the crack beneath. It was not Duffie. He pawed at the front door and whined, to show Kathleen she should open it.

"Well, if you think so—" Kathleen opened it dubiously, just an inch or so.

Robin burst the door the whole way open and threw himself on both of them, shivering and tearful and glad all at once. "I *knew* you'd be here! She was the only Smith who didn't say I'd got the wrong number. Kathleen, please can I stay with you! I want to be with you and Shamus. It's horrible at home with only Basil."

"Hush!" said Kathleen. "Miss Smith's asleep. Come in the warm. You're frozen."

She took Robin into the sitting room. He threw himself into the chair which was a better fit for dogs and burst into tears. "It's been awful!" he said. "They're so angry. And Basil and I had to cook supper in the end, only we burned everything. And that made Basil have a terrible row with Mum and go storming off to look for Remains. And when he didn't come back—"

"Didn't come back?" said Kathleen.

"No," sobbed Robin. "He told them he was going to stay away for good. I think it was really because Mum's going to have the Ra—er, Shamus—put down, only they both pretended it was about the supper. So then Dad and Mum had another row and Dad phoned the police again, and so I had to wait for ages before I could get away. Please let me stay here, Kathleen."

"You can stay till you're warm," said Kathleen. "And then I'll take you back. I'll have to," she said, as Robin wailed. "They'll be mad with worry if you go missing too. But it's me they're angry about. I'll explain to Uncle Harry for you, and I'll stay if you want me to. I knew it was too good to be true, staying with Miss Smith."

Sirius sighed as he listened to Kathleen comforting Robin. That was Kathleen all over. She would spoil all Miss Smith's plans and his own, and go back to be miserable with the Duffields, just because Robin was upset. But at least she was so taken up with Robin that she did not seem to be needing Sirius any more. He thought he could go. He had already got up to leave, when the doorbell rang again, an angry, jabbing trill.

Robin seized Kathleen's arm. "Is it Dad?"

"I'll see." Kathleen braced her shoulders and marched to the door. Sirius followed her. If it was Duffie, he supposed he might have to bite her again.

But it was Basil. He stood on the steps staring rather accusingly at Kathleen. "I saw Robin and trailed him," he said aggressively. "What did you want to go and let him bite Mum for?" Before Sirius could wonder who had bitten whom, Basil pounced past Kathleen and proved he had been talking about Sirius by hugging him crushingly. "Beastly old Rat!" he said, burying his face in Sirius's coat. "She won't let you in the house again now."

Robin arrived in the hall. "How did *he* get here?" he demanded unwelcomingly.

"Quiet!" said Kathleen, shutting the front door and glancing anxiously at the stairs. "Poor Miss Smith was so tired. Come in the sitting room, all of you."

Sirius realized he was not likely to get away at all that night. Basil kept tight hold of him and flopped into the chair Robin had just left, with Sirius pinned between his knees. And Sirius found he was not displeased to see Basil again. His tail wagged itself energetically. "I thought I saw you, Rat," said Basil. "Near the river, where they've knocked a lot of houses down. There was this dog, barking at a man and a woman. They were ever such peculiar types, sort of lit up round the edges, one blue and the other sort of white. I only went near them because I thought it was you barking. And they ran off when I came, and then I saw it wasn't you, it was a dog just like you."

"That must have been Bruce," said Kathleen. Sirius thought so too. It was clear New-Sirius and his Companion had made the same mistake as Basil. Sirius hoped Bruce was safe. "But Basil," said Kathleen, "what did you think you were doing, going off like that?"

Basil went sullen. "I was festering furious. That's why. I was going to stay out all night and scare them properly. I've read hundreds of books where people are up all night. Only," he said resentfully, "they none of them warn you how boring it is. And they say you get tired—but you don't. You just get a sick, hungry sort of feeling and keep on wanting to sit down, and all the cafés close, so you can't get anything to eat. That's why I went home—only I saw Robin come out and followed him instead. Kathleen, have you got anything I can eat?"

Basil seemed so desperate that Kathleen crept to Miss Smith's kitchen and made him a pot of tea and buttered some leftover scones. Sirius pattered mournfully beside her, worried about Bruce and certain that his chance to find the Zoi had gone. He had not the heart to eat the scone Kathleen gave him. He lay with it between his paws in the sitting room while the others ate and drank and talked. It was clear Kathleen was going back to the Duffields. Robin wanted her to. Basil simply assumed that she would. Sirius sighed.

A sudden silence fell. After a while, Sirius looked up to see why. To his surprise, all three of them were asleep, Basil in the dog-shaped chair and Robin and Kathleen packed together in the frayed chair opposite. The room sounded only of heavy breathing and the loud ticking of Miss Smith's eccentric clock. It was the most astonishing piece of luck. Sirius got up and crept to the dog-door. It thumped behind him as he bounded down the garden.

To his relief, the Moon had not yet risen. But he could

feel it near, close to the horizon. He set off at a gallop for the cleared space, in far too much of a hurry to care whether or not his Companion saw him.

The cindery space was dark and quiet, but, from where the bulldozers sat like crippled monsters, a breeze blew a faint scent of ozone and jasmine. It was only faint. Nevertheless, Sirius bent his legs to a crouch and slunk like a dim white cat until he came to the shelter of the first clump of nettles. He slid this way and that among the weeds, hurried and low. And there, at last, was the black heap of rubble breaking in amongst the wheeling stars. He could smell the musky sap of elders. A white coat glinted among the bundles of new leaves. Bruce was there.

"Hallo," Sirius said cautiously.

"Hallo, hallo, hallo!" The white coat surged and the branches parted this way and that. Bruce bounded to meet him. Dim white dogs spurted out of the thicket behind him. The place seemed crowded with milling dogs, all running around him and saying Hallo. Sirius touched noses with Rover, with Redears, with Bruce himself, and with Patchie. Patchie, because she had Rover there with her, was friendlier than any of them.

"What on Earth are you all doing here?" Sirius asked, running round and round with the rest.

"Bruce says there's going to be a hunt," said Redears. "What fun, what fun, what fun!"

"I opened their gates," said Bruce. "Some queer people chased me and I got lonely. I hope you don't mind."

"Not at all," said Sirius, still hardly able to believe it.

The Moon slid softly above the houses.

The cleared space was suddenly new and strange. It was an enchanted mesh of blue shadows and white leaves, and the mounds of rubble stood about in it like crusty old creatures. They looked as if they might wake up and stretch, and scratch where the bushes itched them, at any moment. Every living thing seemed ten times more alive. Patchie sneezed, and Rover growled. Ozone-jasmine and a green scent as strong as the elders flowed across the space, almost drowning the flat white scent of the Moon. A large figure and a small one walked across the level ground. The light of the Moon met and clashed with the blue-green light around one and the pearly light around the other, so that they winked and stretched like candle flames.

"Keep running round and round!" Sirius said desperately.

The other dogs obeyed, rather bewildered. "Is this part of the hunt?" Redears asked.

"Sort of," Sirius answered, running around him and then around Patchie. The two figures had stopped, but he did not think they would be confused for long. Now the Moon had risen, he could see that he and the other dogs were not identical. He and Bruce were indeed very alike, with their long legs and narrow bodies, but Rover and Redears were of a dumpier Labrador build, and Rover was distinctly chubby. Patchie was in between, narrow-bodied like Bruce, but shorter in the legs. Sirius knew that his Companion had only to look at his eyes to tell him apart from the rest.

"One of them must be him," New-Sirius said.

"Don't waste any more time," said his Companion. "I can feel the Zoi near. You'd better kill the lot of them."

New-Sirius raised an arm with blue-green rays winking and stretching around it. At the same moment, there was a fierce fresh pricking from the Zoi. A great dim shape appeared out of nowhere. It might have been a man on horseback, or it might have been something else. Whatever it was, New-Sirius and the Companion were right in its way. New-Sirius turned and struck at it. At least, Sirius thought he did. Blue-green flared and vanished, swallowed up in dimness. Then the great shape knockcd both him and his Companion aside and swept on its way.

Sirius was astonished. No creature, no child of Earth, ought to be strong enough to do that to two luminaries. But there was no time to wonder about it. That sound which was not a sound rang out in a noiseless fanfare. "Follow me, follow me, follow me!" It clamored through Sirius's head, stronger and fiercer even than the tingling, spitting life of the Zoi. And the hunt was on.

Glimmering, frantic, frosty, the cold hounds came pouring into the open. Everything was helter-skelter, gleaming eyes, gleaming coats and the wild pattering of feet, as hundreds of white dogs raced after the dim shape.

"Come on!" said Bruce.

Uncertain whether they were following or pursuing, the five warm dogs bounded in amongst the cold hounds. The hunt took them up and swept them through the cleared space. A moment later, they were streaming pell-mell down the nearest road that led to the river. Sirius supposed New-Sirius and his Companion must be following, but he had no time to think about them.

At the end of the street, by the river, the noiseless noise rang out again and again. "Follow me, follow me!" The dark shape and the pursuing white ones turned upriver and sped along the muddy towpath, strung out and struggling for position. Sirius and Bruce, being the lightest-built of the five, forced their way into the center of the pack and ran there, surrounded by chilly panting bodies, all of which gave off the stinging tingle of creatures that had been near a Zoi. But Sirius almost forgot the Zoi. He was simply glad the hounds were cold. He was hotter than he had ever been in his life. And the weird compelling fanfare kept ringing in his ears, telling him to *follow, follow, follow,* and think of nothing else.

Follow he did, madly, panting and jostling, along the towpath and through the dark railway yard, across railway lines and over jumbled old sleepers. Beyond the engine sheds, they raced beside an iron fence. Through it, Sirius glimpsed a grassy old bridge across the river. Their quarry was already flying across the bridge, with the hounds on its heels. It looked like a great black beast with branched horns. The sight made him want to bay with triumph. But the cold hounds ran silent, and he did not dare make a noise.

The next second, the same dim shape—surely the same: he knew there was only one—was at his side, right beside the racing, struggling pack in which he ran, urging them on to cross the bridge. "Follow me, follow me, follow me!" shouted the urgent fanfare. And Sirius, though he followed frantically, was suddenly terrified in case the great beast was caught. Yet he rushed across the old bridge and plunged after it between the houses beyond.

After the houses, they were in open country. And there Sirius found that the hunt up to now had hardly been in earnest. Out in the fields, they ran more madly still. They raced over sprouting corn with the white Moon over them and their black Moon-shadows flickering underneath. They poured around dark copses where bats flittered and owls wheeled above them. They leaped fences, tore through hedges and struggled in and out of ditches, regarding nothing but that noiseless sound calling them on, on, on after the dim shape. Sometimes the sound was dim and urgent out in front. Sometimes it was at their side. Sirius ran in a daze and in a muddle. Once or twice, in the early stages of the hunt, he scented ozone-jasmine faintly. But it soon vanished. Sirius hardly noticed. He was trying too hard to understand whether they were with the quarry or after it.

The muddle grew worse. Sirius did not understand what he wanted. Their quarry raced and looped and doubled. It led them in a desperate circle around a black clump of trees, and they almost lost it. Sirius, with all the other hounds, cast about in a frenzy, afraid they had lost it for good. Yet, at the same time, he was overjoyed that it had got away.

It was Bruce who found the right scent. "Here! This way! Oh, I do hope we don't catch him!" And he led the hunt streaming away over the silvery brow of a hill, hot on the trail of the beast, agog for its blood, and madly wanting it to escape.

The dim beast evaded them several times more. Each time they were after it quicker, pell-mell, more savagely, and each time Sirius hoped harder it would escape. Mile after mile, his feelings became more of a muddle. He wanted to stop and think, but he could not, because, each time he paused, the dim shape itself came dashing past the silent pack and the soundless noise shouted "Follow me, follow me!" And they had to follow. Sirius began to hate it with a sort of tender terror.

And at last, in the middle of a field, miles from anywhere, they caught it and pulled it down. It was a mad heap of white bodies and fighting black shadow, and Sirius ran around it, savage with sorrow and frantic with triumph. The heap subsided to a flat blot of milling dogs, all tearing and pulling at something. The soundless noise rang out again from underneath, only this time it said, "The kill, the kill, the kill!"

A queer cold lump of meat came to Sirius—he did not know how. He fell on it furiously and ate it guiltily. Beside him, Bruce, Redears and Yeff snarled and tore at lumps of their own. Then, when every scrap was eaten, they all lay down, cold and panting under the sinking Moon, because something had ordered them to rest. Sirius had never felt so wretched and so triumphant in his life.

"What does all this mean?" he asked the Moon.

"Hush," said the Moon. "You'll see."

Of a sudden, they were up again. First up was the great dim shape. It went flying back across the field, summoning them all to *follow, follow*. Sirius saw—though he did not understand in the least—that Master and quarry were indeed one and the same. He knew they had just eaten him, yet there he was, and they were chasing him, cold dogs and warm dogs alike. Sirius raced after the dim shape, trying to see what manner of being it was. He could not tell. But, in an odd way, he no longer wondered why Earth had gone to such trouble to help this being. Sirius found he wanted to help him, himself. It was not the soundless call which made him follow so fast now: it was a peculiar fierce pity.

The hunt went streaming back toward town. Meanwhile, in Miss Smith's house, Kathleen woke up. In her sleep, she had heard the dog-door thump and the gate whine and click as Sirius left, and she had been waiting, in her sleep, to hear the same again in reverse, meaning Leo was back. When she did not hear it, she woke up.

"Robin! I think Leo's run away!"

Robin and Basil both jumped awake and stared around Miss Smith's unfamiliar room, wondering why it had come there instead of their bedrooms. "He can't have done!" Robin said sleepily, and Basil said, "Why would he?" while he tried to get the crick out of his neck.

"Because he heard me say I was going back home with you," Kathleen explained impatiently. "He thought he was going to be destroyed."

Robin accepted that without question and levered himself out of the chair. "We'd better go and look for him."

"But he doesn't understand that kind of thing!" Basil said crossly. He wanted to go back to sleep.

"Yes, he does," Kathleen assured him. "He knew what Duffie meant after he bit her. And when I had to tell Duffie I was going to take him to the vet myself, he wouldn't move until I told him I wasn't."

Basil believed her. He privately knew the Rat was exceptional anyway. But he still wanted to go back to sleep. "How could we ever find him?" he asked contemptuously.

"I think he's gone with Bruce," said Kathleen. "You saw Bruce earlier on, Basil. Take us to where you saw him."

In spite of Basil's grumbles, she borrowed Miss Smith's pen and wrote her a note in case she was worried. *Basil and Robin and me have gone after Leo and Bruce down near the river. Love, Kathleen.* While she was writing it, Robin crept sleepily into every room in Miss Smith's house, just to make sure Shamus was not asleep on a bed or somewhere. But he was not. So they let themselves quietly out of the house.

They were all three no more than half awake. What they were doing seemed as logical to them as the things you do in dreams. They were too sleepy to notice it was cold outside, and the empty echoes in the street simply added to the dreamlike feeling. So did the lit-up deserted shops, the late yellow Moon, and the way the street lights and the moonlight doubled and sometimes tripled the shadows stretching from their clopping feet. When their feet stopped clopping and crunched on cinders, and the only light was from the Moon, it felt like another phase of the dream. None of them was alarmed when they saw a man and a woman slip out of sight behind a bank of rubble. It was odd, but natural, the way it is in dreams, that the man was outlined in faint turquoise light and the woman in white.

"Those are the people the dog was barking at," Basil remarked. "It was along here, where it's all overgrown. I'll show you." He led the way beyond the bank of rubble. Weeds looped across their feet. They stumbled on concealed bricks and dimly noticed that they were being stung by nettles, but it was still all like a dream.

It was even more like a dream when the wild hunt swept toward them. They heard a furious frosty pattering and turned to look. The great dark shape in front was bearing down on them. They got out of its way as fast as they could. But, before they could feel frightened, the shining white hounds came leaping and pouring after it, more and more and faster and faster. They watched, dizzy and fascinated.

"I think it means bad luck," Robin remarked dubiously.

"There's *Leo!*" shrieked Kathleen.

"Where?" said Basil.

"There! There!" said Kathleen. She stumbled forward into the whirling crowd of dogs. They simply divided and ran around her, cold and fast as a foaming river. But Kathleen saw a dog with a collar go by and managed to catch hold of it. Bruce went on running with the rest, and Kathleen was swept across the cleared space with him.

"That's not the Rat," Basil said scornfully.

The dizzying line was coming to an end. The last dogs were fewer and slower. Redears and Patchie came laboring by, footsore and draggled, only running still because the unheard fanfare was ringing out and making them follow. Robin seized Patchie's collar.

"Catch hold!" he called to Basil. "We'll find Shamus when they stop."

Rover came last of all, limping, almost done up. Basil snatched hold of Rover's collar and ran with him after the rest. It was probable that, without Basil to pull him, Rover would not have covered the last few yards. But he made it, and ran with Basil into nothingness.

15 THE UNDERWORLD—if that was what it was—seemed to Sirius to be a cool, dim place. He did not notice much of it, except that the ground was cold and soft and bright green, like moss, the ideal surface for his sore and weary paws. He was too tired to look further, or even to make plans. Like all the other dogs around him, he simply threw himself down on the soft green stuff and set about going to sleep.

Almost at once, his aching body fizzed and tingled like new life coming into a numb leg. For a second or so, he thought it must be some virtue in the green stuff. Then he recognized the Zoi, very strong and very near. It put such life into him that he stirred and raised his tired head.

The dog next to him snarled. "Warm—this one's warm!"

Weary dog heads came up all around him. The only light in the place seemed to be coming from the moss-stuff itself, underneath them. Each of them looked like a fierce white gargoyle, with ears of blood and eyes like lamps. "It's wearing a collar," one said. "It's a filthy impostor!"

Sirius recognized Yeff. "Yeff," he said, "you told me it would be all right if I ran with you."

"I told you no such thing, mongrel!" snapped Yeff, and heaved to his feet. "Come on, all of you. Kill it!"

Tired and slow and bad-tempered, the dogs around Sirius heaved up too, growling and snarling. Sirius scrambled to his sore feet and did his best to snarl back. As they went for him, he heard snarls and yelps beyond, where Bruce and then Patchie were discovered. Rover, in the distance, was yelping, "Save us, save us, save us!" at the top of his powerful voice. The uproar grew. Sirius thought he heard a human scream as part of it, but he was too busy defending himself to attend. Yeff had him by the ear, and another dog was snatching at his throat.

A voice spoke nearby. "What is going on?" it said wearily. It was a dark voice, flat as a cracked bell, as deep and gloomy as the sound of wind in a hollow corner. It did not seem loud. Nevertheless, the noise stopped at once. The dogs around Sirius crawled aside, frightened and abashed. "Lie down all of you," said the Master of the hunt, "and go to sleep."

Sirius was astonished at the force of that command. Every creature around him, and away into the dim distance, at once lay down and fell asleep. Sirius nearly did himself. He was dog-tired. He only disobeyed the command by bracing his whole green nature against it. Shakily and slowly, he staggered over the yielding ground toward the Master of the hunt. He was sure he could not have done that had it not been for the Zoi, humming fresh life into him from somewhere nearby.

"What are you?" said the flat hollow voice.

As it spoke, the command seemed to be lifted. Sirius made his way between cold sleeping hounds until he was standing in front of their Master. The dim figure seemed to be man-shaped now. At least, Sirius saw only two shadowy legs standing on the glowing moss. The rest was hard to see, since light only came from the ground, but Sirius looked up, searching where the Master's head seemed to flare away into shadow, and caught a glimpse of eyes, round and liquid, with a tinge of red to them. But the shadowy arm went up to cover the eyes as Sirius looked into them.

"What are you?" the hollow voice repeated.

Sirius was certain that he was standing in front of a power as great, or greater, than any he had known. He could not understand how Earth came to have such a child as this, nor why he should hide his eyes. He felt a good deal of respect, and also the same fierce pity he had felt as they raced back to town. "I used to be a luminary," he said. "And I need to talk to you."

"I'm not sure I need to talk to you," the Master answered. "Luminaries take their powers from light. Mine come from darkness. We can only do one another harm."

"But I ran with your hounds so that I could talk to you," said Sirius. "I don't think you can refuse."

"No," said the Master. "I can't. But——"

"Talk to him," Earth said suddenly, in a whisper out of the green moss. "He knows how to use the Zoi."

"Does he?" said the Master. There was interest in his flat voice. "Come with me, then," he said to Sirius. He turned like a wheeling shadow and led the way along the mass of sleeping dogs. Sirius found, as he plodded over the chilly moss behind him, that the light which came from it seemed only to light the little circle in which they went. Everything beyond was dim. But the Master could evidently see beyond the circle. He seemed to be searching among the sleeping dogs as he went. First Bruce, then Redears and Patchie, and finally Rover, got up and limped over to them as they passed. "Your brothers and sister are only ordinary dogs, luminary," the Master said. "Why is that?"

"I don't really know," Sirius confessed.

The Master stood still. "And who are these?"

"Oh," said Patchie, peering around him. "Dead people."

Beyond the dogs, Kathleen, Robin and Basil were curled up asleep on the moss. They lay so still that Sirius thought at first that Patchie was right. He rushed at Kathleen and nosed her. To his relief, she was warm and moved sleepily away from the cold nose on her face. "Leo," she mumbled.

"Is she your mistress?" asked the Master of the hunt.

"Yes, that's Kathleen," Sirius said.

"They'll be all right," said the Master. "Come over here, all of you."

A little farther on, the feeling from the Zoi was stingingly sharp. The other dogs felt it as well as Sirius, and shook themselves uncomfortably. Meanwhile, the Master sat down in a place where the green stuff was mounded up into the form of a chair. As he sat in it, Sirius noticed that it moved and eased around him to make him as comfortable as possible. Near the chair, the moss had sunk itself into a hollow to make a kind of pen for a red-eared white bitch and a tumbling mass of frosty white puppies. Seeing the strange dogs, the mother rose up growling and glaring to warn them off. The puppies behaved just like the fox cubs. They tried to climb the steep mossy sides of their pen, squealing to be played with and yelping with frustration when the Master put out a shadowy arm and rolled them back to their mother.

The Master was no easier to see sitting than he had been standing. He was nothing but a flaring gloom. Out of the gloom, the sad, liquid eyes were turned on the four ordinary dogs crouched in front of his chair. "You ran with my hunt," he said to them. "What is it you want?"

Bruce looked at Sirius to see if he still wanted him to ask for the Zoi, but, while he was looking, Redears said, "We don't want much. We just want to be sure of not getting into trouble when we get home."

"Yes, that's what we want," Patchie and Rover agreed. And Bruce said, "Particularly me. I've been out two days now."

"I think I can let you have that," said the Master. There was some amusement in his hollow voice.

"Thank you," they said gratefully, and they settled down side by side to rest. "You do understand, don't you?" Bruce said to Sirius before he fell asleep.

"Now," said the Master to Sirius, and he stretched out an arm. A dim finger pointed to a place in the moss about a yard away from Sirius. It opened like a green mouth. Like a tongue coming out, a green hummock rose from the opening, carrying with it a scaly purple-gray stone about a foot long. It looked like a cinder in the shape of a pine cone, except that it was heavy. It dented the green moss where it lay.

Sirius had never seen a Zoi look like that before. But he knew it at once, and knew that this must be the form of it best fitted for Earth. His nose turned to it as it might turn into a wind. His tail curled stiffly up behind him. He went slowly toward it, almost unable to believe he had found it at last.

And he was stopped. A foot away from the hummock he could not get any nearer to it. He ran around it to try from the other side, and it was the same there. "What are you doing?" he asked the Master.

"It killed the hound that found it," he answered. "I've not let any creature touch it since. But I could see it was a thing of great power, so I kept it, hoping I could find a way to use it. You tell me, luminary. What is it, this Zoi?"

Sirius sat down, with his nose toward the vibrant dry cinder he so much wanted, and tried to explain. "If you think of all power as a kind of movement," he said, "then a Zoi is composed of the movement behind the movement.

It's the stuff of life itself, it—"

"If it's made of movement," the Master interrupted, "that explains why I can't use it."

Sirius was astonished. "I'd have thought you had the power. Why not?"

The Master shook his great head. For a moment, Sirius had a feeling that tall, branched antlers swayed above it. "No, darkness is not movement," he said somberly. "Nor is the other part of my power, which comes from things as they must be. I'm stronger than you are, luminary, but I can't use the Zoi. It's a different order of being."

"How did you come to be a child of Earth's?" Sirius demanded.

"Earth has the seeds of everything," said the Master. "Tell me what this Zoi can do."

"Well, everything," said Sirius. "Everything that is movement, anyway. It can make or change anything, give life or take it away, take something to the other end of space and fetch it back—"

The mother dog growled again. Sirius looked around and saw that Robin was leaning over the side of the hollow, gazing yearningly at the puppies.

"Oh, I want one!" he said to Basil, who was kneeling just beyond him.

Basil was looking at the Zoi. It was obvious he could think of nothing else. "That's that meteorite," he·said. "I know it is. Isn't it a beauty?"

Kathleen was awake too. She was sitting on the moss watching Sirius in a puzzled way. When he looked at her, she got up and came to pat him. "Leo, you silly dog! You're worn out!" Then she turned to the Master of the hunt, meaning to apologize for coming into his private place after her dog. She met his half-seen liquid eyes. Then her own eyes went upward to the dark space above his head, where surely a pair of antlers stood like two dim horny trees. "I'm sorry," she said. It was all she meant to say. She said it in much the same way as she had refused to open the gate for Sirius.

The Master said uneasily, "Don't look too closely. The truth has no particular shape."

"I know that," Kathleen said, rather impatiently. Her eyes stayed watching the space above the Master's head for all that. "But you're not Arawn, are you?" she said.

The boys had seen the Master for the first time. They were both terrified. Robin's teeth chattered and he said, "But he could be Orion or Actaeon, couldn't he?"

"Or John Peel," Basil said, very derisively because he was so scared.

Sirius wondered what the three humans had understood about the Master that he had not. It was clear that the Master knew they had understood it, by the way he changed the subject. "You all ran with my hounds," he said.

"Only a very little way," Kathleen said, quickly and firmly.

"But that entitles you to ask one thing of me," the Master told them. "What do you want?"

Sirius pricked up his ears, knowing he could ask for the Zoi. Kathleen looked eager, then doubtful. Robin swung around and pointed delightedly at the hollow full of tumbling white puppies. "Then, could I—?"

"I want that meteorite," Basil said loudly. "If we can have one thing, then we ought to have that, because it's the *only* way I can get it. I need it. So don't either of you go and be selfish."

Kathleen and Robin exchanged wistful looks. Robin sighed. "All right."

"I meant one thing each," said the Master.

Robin was transformed into delight again. "In that case, can I have one of those puppies, please?"

"Certainly. When you leave here," said the Master. "But," he said to Basil, "I don't think I shall be able to give you your meteorite."

"Why not?" Basil demanded angrily. "It's not fair!"

"If you were to give me the Zoi," Sirius said, for once in his life glad that Basil could not understand him, "I could make him a meteorite exactly like that in a second. He wouldn't know the difference."

"That would be the solution," the Master agreed, and turned to Kathleen. "And you?"

"Leo *is* talking to you!" Kathleen exclaimed. "I thought he was before. And you can understand him, can't you? And I can't. I've tried and Leo's tried, but we can't. How do you do it?"

"I can understand him because neither of us is human," the Master said. His flat gloomy voice became flatter and gloomier. "If you really wish it, it can be brought about that you and your dog understand one another, but I think you might regret it. Is that what you want?"

"Yes," Kathleen said recklessly.

"Ask for something else," said the Master.

Kathleen was puzzled and uneasy. "But there's only one other thing I couldn't get in an ordinary way—and I know I can't ask you that," she said. "I won't ask for anything, then."

There was a short silence. Then the Master said, "No. Have what you asked for. You can all have what you want, but I think two of you are very unwise to ask. Do you really want the Zoi, luminary?"

"I have to have it," Sirius said. "You don't understand— it's harming Sol's system."

"I care very little for Sol," said the Master. "As little as he cares for me. But you can have it if you want. Meanwhile, there's something you can do for me." He leaned forward and picked the Zoi off its cushion of green moss. Basil's eyes followed it as well as Sirius's. After what the Master had said, Sirius was not surprised to see the Zoi blur and shrink between his shadowy fingers. The prickling life of it stopped entirely, and there was a dead kind of peace. "I don't find it comfortable to hold," the Master remarked. "You hold it for me." To the terror of Sirius and the annoyance of Basil, he passed it to Kathleen.

"Hey!" said Basil.

Sirius jumped forward to try to take the Zoi himself, sure that it would kill Kathleen to touch it. The Zoi was heavy. Kathleen's hands dipped under it and he almost got it. But Kathleen said, "No, Leo," and raised it high out of his reach. Sirius jumped anxiously around her, rather astonished that the Zoi did not seem to harm her, and Basil hovered jealously at Kathleen's elbow.

"He said I could have it."

"You shall have it presently," said the Master of the hunt. "Kathleen, do you think you can make that thing work?"

Kathleen, very puzzled, turned the Zoi over and looked at either end. She seemed quite unharmed by it. The prickling life of it did not seem as strong as before the Master picked it up. Sirius suspected that, though the Master of the hunt could not use the Zoi himself, he was able to protect Kathleen from the effects of it. "How does it work?" Kathleen asked. "There aren't any switches."

"Meteorites don't have switches, you festering idiot!" Basil said. "They don't—"

The green ground underneath them shook. There was a queer noise, like cloth slowly tearing. The mother dog growled. Patchie and her brothers opened their eyes and stared around. Sirius thought at first that the Zoi was responsible, until everyone turned toward the dim empty distance beyond the Master's chair.

There was a strong smell of singeing and the dimness seemed to be bulging inwards. A gray light, with a hint of blue-green, was shining through the bulge, and it was increasing piece by piece, as if someone was tearing a way through. From the noise, someone was doing just that. Sirius took one look and darted in between Rover and Redears. He lay down, half turned away from the tearing, and pretended to be asleep. It was the only way of hiding he could think of.

New-Sirius and his Companion, with light limning their human shapes, trudged across the green ground. It went writhing away from under their feet, so that they walked in a smoking black scar of bare Earth. The smoke from it made everyone cough, except the Master of the hunt. Behind the two luminaries was white morning mist, dripping nettles and wet grass, making a queer contrast with the light from the green floor.

"We want that dog," said New-Sirius. "Give him up to us, and nobody will get hurt."

"There's the Zoi, too," said the Companion, pointing at Kathleen. "We'll have that as well."

They came on, bringing the mist and weeds outside nearer and nearer. The poor mother dog stood in the smoke above her puppies and snarled at them. The children stared, not understanding at all. The Master stood up. The new light made him harder to see than ever. But that was only for an instant. As soon as he was on his feet, the outside world was gone again. The green moss healed and spread itself into the distance, until the only burned part left was where the two luminaries were standing.

"This is my place," the Master said in his flat somber voice. "You can't come here."

"Oh, yes we can," said New-Sirius. "Earth is part of my sphere. I govern this whole system."

"But not me," said the Master.

"Nonsense!" said the Companion. "You're only one of

Earth's creatures. Hand over the dog and the Zoi, before we have to make you."

"And you won't like that," said New-Sirius. He took a step toward the Master, or, rather, he intended to. But he remained in the same burned spot. He leaned forward and tried again. He still could not move. "You can't do this!" he said incredulously. "We're luminaries."

His Companion threw herself forward and beat her white fists on nothing. "Stop this at once! How *dare* you!"

The Master said nothing and did not move. The anger of both luminaries blazed in sheets about them and flared uselessly away into dimness.

"Do you think it's some kind of force-field?" Basil said to Robin.

"I don't understand. What do they want?" said Kathleen.

The Master's great branched head turned toward her. "They want to kill your dog."

"Leo?" said Kathleen, clutching the Zoi to her chest. "They're not going to kill Leo! I'll see them dead first!"

The prickle of the Zoi suddenly became the sweet sting of force truly used. Sirius felt his coat stand and wave as the power of the Zoi swept across it. He turned in time to see his Companion throw up her arm against it. It did no good. She, and her new Consort with her, were already diminishing as she moved. Side by side they dwindled steadily and, as they shrunk, they seemed to move farther off. When both seemed a foot high, it was impossible to tell if they were small near-to or huge a million miles away. Sirius was reminded of the time he first saw Sol go. In a second, the two luminaries were only a greenish speck and a whitish one, dwindling and receding still. Then they were gone, too small to see.

"Just like when they turn off the television," Bruce remarked to Sirius.

"I did that, didn't I?" Kathleen said. "They were horrible anyway, but where have they gone?"

"Who knows?" said the Master of the hunt. "But now you can use that thing, will you use it for me?"

"How is Kathleen able to use a Zoi?" Sirius demanded.

"Being a child of Earth means more than you think," said the Master. "Kathleen, I want you to use the Zoi to change my situation. I'm sick of being a child of night. My ancestors came out by day and didn't frighten or puzzle people. I want to be the same."

"How do you mean?" said Kathleen.

"Your dog can tell you how he felt when he ran with my hounds," said the Master. "He was cruel and kind at once. It must have muddled him. Isn't that so?" he asked Sirius.

"Yes," said Sirius, and he began trying to explain to Kathleen about the queer muddle of sympathy and savagery he had felt. But he stopped, because Kathleen had not understood a word. She was nearly in tears about it.

"I know he's talking, but I still can't understand. You promised I could!"

"You've cheated her!" said Sirius. "Are you planning to cheat me over the Zoi, too?"

"I never cheat," said the Master. "You've cheated yourselves. I promised, and I warned you both, and I shall keep that promise. Kathleen, use the Zoi for me. I want to walk Earth as you do."

"I don't think you should," said Kathleen. "Not if you're going to cheat and muddle everyone."

"I only do that because I'm in darkness," said the Master. "Can't you understand?"

He came toward Kathleen. Perhaps he meant to show her what he was talking about. At any rate, the dimness from him fell over her, almost blotting her out. Kathleen backed out from it, terrified.

"No, no," she said. "Don't come near me. Don't do that!" The Zoi, as she clutched it, once more gave out its sweet sting of force, and the dim green space rang with its power.

"I knew this would happen once the veil was torn," the Master of hounds said, and folded his arms. Then, quietly, without any of them noticing, he was not there anymore. The rest of the place went with him. There was no green moss, no mother dog, no pack of cold hounds sleeping. The ground, rough and full of bricks, slanted under their feet, and they found they were standing halfway up the mound of rubble where Sirius had lost Yeff. It was all cold and colorless in the time just before sunrise. The damp, misty air made them shiver. And all around in the mist, they could hear people moving, calling to one another and whistling, and dogs barking.

16 THE FOUR TRUE dogs stood with their heads on one side and one paw raised, listening. "Goodness!" said Bruce. "That's my master whistling!"

"And mine," said Patchie, Rover and Redears.

"If you don't mind," said Bruce, "I think we ought to be off now. So long."

They were all off, without more ado, into the wet whiteness. Some of the calling and whistling stopped and became relieved cries of "There you are, you bad dog!" But most of it went on.

"What's going on?" Robin said sleepily. He went up the mound, stumbling from brick to brick, to see what the noise was about. Near the top, he shouted with delight. "Look! Look! He remembered!" The Master of hounds had kept this promise at least. A fat white puppy with blood-red ears was stumbling about up there, cheeping for its mother. Robin picked it up tenderly. Finding it was frosty cold, he wrapped it in his sweater and sat down with it, trying in a puzzled way to warm it up.

"Right," said Basil. "He's got his. Give me my meteorite."

Kathleen held the Zoi to her and clambered away from Basil, backwards up the mound. "It isn't a proper meteorite. It's dangerous. I don't think you should have it."

"He *promised* me!" Basil said, climbing furiously after her.

Sirius bounded up with him and pranced around Kathleen, trying to show her she should give it to him instead. But Kathleen raised the Zoi out of his reach. "No, Leo. It's a horribly strong thing. You're not having it either."

"Give it me!" shouted Basil. Kathleen ran away from him, to the top of the mound. Basil caught her there and tried to twist the Zoi out of her hand. They wrestled for it, to and fro, just above Robin's head, while Robin sat absorbed in his puppy. Basil of course was the stronger. Sirius jumped around him, getting in his way, barging Basil's legs whenever he could. He did not like to think what would happen if Basil touched the Zoi. Nor did he quite trust Kathleen not to use it again by accident. Basil gripped Kathleen's arm and twisted it back. Sirius barged at his elbow. It was a hideously familiar sight. He and his Companion had wrestled for the Zoi exactly like this, and he was afraid it was going to be lost again, or destroy them all.

The bump Sirius gave Basil loosened Kathleen's fingers. The Zoi fell from her hand and went plummeting to Earth. Since it was not made of the same stuff as Sol's system, it fell like a streak of light. Sirius leaped for it. He was only just in time to catch it in his mouth before it entered the ground.

It hurt him. He had not known anything could hurt so much. The pain started at his mouth and spread all over him like a green flame. It was as much as he could do to make Basil another cindery cone, falling at an ordinary speed. After that, he could think of nothing but how much it hurt.

The heavy cinder thumped down on the bricks. Basil rushed at it and scooped it up. He glared at Kathleen. "I told you it was mine!" he said. Then he ran away down the mound with it in case Kathleen tried to get it again.

The pain did not last long. Sirius stood up out of it and stretched, light and liquid and free. He was a reasonable size again. He found himself looking down over Kathleen, out across the white mist that hung over the cleared space. Police cars with lights on were parked on the cinders. Policemen with dogs and torches were busily searching through the rubble and the nettles. He saw Mr. Duffield with them, and Miss Smith leaning anxiously out of one of the police cars. But they were only little details at the edges of his great green freedom. The warm, stupid dog was gone. Better still, there was a lightness and power at his shoulders. He had been without his wings so long that he had almost forgotten what they felt like. He spread and shook them, so that the silvery-green flames of the pinions streamed and whispered behind him. He would have wagged his tail with pleasure, except that he no longer had a tail. Instead, he took the Zoi out of his mouth and laughed down at Kathleen. Somehow, he had no doubt that she would be able to understand him now.

"It feels marvelous!" he said.

Kathleen did understand him. She raised her head. Her eyes climbed wonderingly up this sudden green giant, paused on his fierce silver-green face, and moved on over the mane of dense flame-like hair to the huge double wings at his back. Compared with this being, the Master of the hunt now struck her as small and tame. Wondering where he had come from, she said politely, "Does it? I'm so glad."

Sirius was puzzled, and rather hurt. "Don't you know me?"

Kathleen raised her face again. "I don't think so," she said in the same polite way. "Are you an angel?"

"Of course not!" he said. "I'm Sirius. I've been your dog for a year. You must know me!"

"Oh," said Kathleen, and she looked down again.

Sirius looked to see what was taking her attention so thoroughly. There was a big dog in the mist at his feet, lying on its side in the weeds. It was a young dog, rather too thin, with a cream-colored coat and reddish ears. The ear he could see had recently been bitten. The dog was dead. He could see that from the drying skin on its pale eyes, even though it was still twitching a little from the life that had been in it. He looked at Kathleen's stiff face and he knew what the Master of the hunt had been warning them of. Perhaps this was why he had given the Zoi to Kathleen and not to him.

"Listen," he said. "I'm still the same. I was that dog. Don't you understand?"

Kathleen nodded, though he did not think she really understood. She said, "You don't look like Leo," and then added kindly, "But you look very nice, of course."

Sirius could not bear the look on her face as she turned back to the dog. He held the Zoi out to her. "Take this," he said. "See if you can bring the dog to life again."

But Kathleen put her hands behind her back and backed away. "Oh no, that's quite all right," she said politely.

"Then I'll try," said Sirius, exasperated by Kathleen's polite, distant manner.

"No, really," said Kathleen. "You don't have to bother. It wouldn't be the same."

"Blast that!" said Sirius, and turned the Zoi on the twitching body. Nothing happened. The Zoi hummed and fizzed in its usual way, but there was no sweet sting of force. Sirius exclaimed with annoyance, although he understood well enough. The dog had been himself. The one thing you could not do with a Zoi was use it on yourself. "You'll have to do it," he said to Kathleen. "Here."

He pushed the Zoi at Kathleen's face to make her take it. Kathleen gasped and turned her face away. He heard her hair sizzle. Sirius backed away, horrified. As he went, he saw that the dog's coat had singed and the damp grass under his feet was steaming and smoking. It dawned on him that he could not even touch Kathleen now. True, he could contain his heat, as his Companion and New-Sirius had done, but it was not a thing he had ever been very good at. He did not think he could do it well enough to risk going near Kathleen. He could not lick her face any more. Kathleen could not hug him, in that uncomfortable way of hers, until his back ached and he had to wriggle. She did not even really want to talk to him. All she wanted to do was to look at the dead dog on the ground.

Then Sirius glimpsed a little of the meaning behind the

wild hunt. He had been cruel to Kathleen while he thought he was being kind. Because he had not thought of anything but the Zoi, he had done something worse than Duffie and worse than shooting her father. It did not help to find he had done it to himself too; or that Kathleen, in the kindest possible way, had done exactly the same.

"I'm afraid I cheated you," he said.

"Oh, that's all right," Kathleen said politely, still looking at the dog.

It was only twitching faintly now. Sirius saw that if he was to go back into it, he would have to do it soon. It was no good giving the Zoi to Kathleen. Even if she would take it, he had already made it far too hot for her to hold. Somebody else would have to do it.

"Earth," he said. "Could you take the Zoi and—?"

"I'm sorry," Earth said regretfully. "I only know how to give life once."

That left only Sol. Sirius looked around for him. The mist was pearly pink below. In it, the gray shapes of policemen and their well-meaning dogs were going round and round, trying to puzzle out the most confusing scents they had ever met. The sky above them, over the houses, was pink too, but Sol was still below the horizon.

"Fetch Sol, quickly!" he said to Earth.

"I'm turning as fast as I'm allowed to," said Earth.

Sirius dared not leave that cooling dog. He had to wait. And it seemed to him that Sol would never rise that day.

Sol came at last. He stepped up above the roofs in a bright bundle of spiky beams, turning the wet slates into sheets of silver and the mist into glory.

"Sol," Sirius said desperately.

Sol took one golden glance. "Oh, I see," he said. "So you found it."

"Yes, and here it is," Sirius said, holding the Zoi out to him. "Take it and put me back into that dog again. Quickly!"

"I can try," Sol said dubiously. "But I've never handled a Zoi before."

"Take it," said Sirius. "Put me *back!*"

"All right," said Sol. Kathleen looked up, blinking, as he stretched out a hot yellow arm and Sirius put the Zoi in his hand. She shaded her eyes to look at the bright figure, that was either very near or very far away, standing just above the houses meditatively holding the Zoi. After a moment, the Zoi fired to a bright lump between his white-hot fingers.

Nothing happened.

"Put me back," said Sirius. "What are you doing?"

"I'm trying," said Sol. "I see how to use it. But I'm sorry. I don't think I can put you back."

"Why can't you? You must!" Sirius shouted at him. Sol simply shrugged. Sirius raised his wings and blazed with such rage that several policemen looked up and remarked on the queer green light there was this morning. *"Put me back!"*

"I can't," said Sol. "Could you do it?"

"No," said Sirius. "But that's beside the point. Do it!"

His anger and Sol's light were drying the mist away. A

policeman saw Basil crouching possessively over his meteorite and shouted, "Here's one of the lads!"

"I've told you I can't," said Sol.

"Blast you!" Sirius roared. Then he noticed that Kathleen was staring at him in a wan, horrified way. He must be frightening her out of her wits. He did his best to settle his blazing pinions and smooth his flaming hair, and knelt down so that he would not seem so appallingly tall to her. "Sol says he can't put me back into your dog," he told her. "I'm sorry."

"I know. I heard him," said Kathleen. "You know, I really do believe you *were* inside Leo. His eyes used to look just the same when he was angry."

"I'd go back if I could," said Sirius.

"But I told you it wouldn't be the same," said Kathleen. "Leo would only die again when you left, wouldn't he? It's perfectly all right. Thank you for being so kind. I must go now. I think those policemen are looking for us, and I'd better tell them Robin's gone to sleep over his puppy. Goodby." She smiled at Sirius politely, before she turned and went carefully down the side of the mound.

Sirius stared after her. "What can I do?"

"Nothing," said Earth.

"Come away," Sol suggested, and held down a hand to help him into the empyrean.

Sirius spread his nearly forgotten wings and came up beside Sol. He felt strange and raw. It was darker than he remembered, and the noises astonished him for a moment. Space sang. There were great slow notes, high sweet sounds

—every note in human music and more beside, all winding, twining, combining, and ringing out solemn and single, like a constantly changing tune. It was the sound the spheres made as they turned, and he had almost forgotten it. Feeling stranger than ever, he began to walk the way he supposed was homeward, toward the green sphere. Sol left his own sphere and walked beside him. Sirius knew how conscientious Sol was, and realized Sol was doing him a great honor.

"Should I be going this way?" he said. "New-Sirius is Denizen now, isn't he?"

"Well, no," said Sol. "Not any longer. Your Companion isn't there either, I'm afraid. Polaris sent word just before I dawned on your town that someone had used a Zoi to—er—wipe them out. Both spheres are standing empty now. Who did it?"

"Kathleen," said Sirius. "She didn't know."

"So you can take back your sphere," said Sol, "and start looking for another Companion."

"I'm not having another Companion," said Sirius. "And I'm not having Kathleen in trouble over it, either."

"She won't be," said Sol. "Not if I have anything to say about it. She's one of my creatures, and she was no more used to a Zoi than I am—here it is, by the way. Anyway, Polaris is vouching for us. Most of this was his doing. I wish he'd *told* me, but he was probably right not to. I can't keep secrets. He saw where the Zoi fell, and when he couldn't find it himself, he had you put as near to the place as he could, because he was sure you were covering up for your Companion."

"But he was one of the Judges!" Sirius protested.

"Yes. But they were all three in it," said Sol. "It was as irregular as Pluto's orbit and there's going to be an outcry from the Castor luminaries, and probably from other quarters too, but at least they've got my evidence now. Polaris says you were so flaming loyal that they weren't going to get any evidence against your Companion any other way. I still think they should have *told* me. If I'd known, I would have recognized her when she was trying to get you drowned. Then none of the rest need have happened."

"The Zoi would have been lost, though," said Sirius.

"I'd have got it out of Earth in the end," said Sol. "I'm not pleased with Earth—risking an Ice Age, acting dumb with me, and lying to Polaris like that!"

"Don't be too angry," said Sirius.

"Earth," said Sol, glancing suspicious beams on him, "is mine. To do what I like with."

"I know, I know," Sirius said hastily. "I only meant that Earth was protecting a very strange child. I still don't understand what he was, but he was stronger than any Zoi. Earth may have had no choice."

Before Sol could reply, Polaris came down to meet them, holding out a hand to Sirius and smiling his likable smile. His brothers from the Big Dipper came too, and so did Antares, Betelgeuse and many more, all delighted to see Sirius again. For a moment, Sirius felt he could not face them. He looked back at Earth to steady himself. There, he saw that Miss Smith, after some argument with Mr. Duffield, had taken charge of Kathleen. A police car was taking them both back to Miss Smith's house, on whose door Sirius had battered so often. It seemed the best thing to have happened. He wished he could have done more for her.

With Sol's help, he was able to do one more thing for Kathleen. It was in September, just before she went back to school. Kathleen was taller and browner and outwardly happier. Miss Smith had taken her to France all summer for a complete change. Now she was back, and out shopping for Miss Smith. She had lost her ability to see or understand luminaries, because, of course, that was not what she had asked the Master of the hunt for.

Nevertheless, Sol and Sirius managed, by gentle degrees, to lead her toward the river. They found she still would not go anywhere near what had once been the overgrown cleared space, in spite of the fact that it was quite different these days, with houses, flats and a new school going up all over it. They were forced to lead her on a long detour along the towpath. Sirius was forcibly reminded of himself as a dog, when he had to nudge and push and hint Kathleen to go where he wanted.

They nudged and pushed and hinted Kathleen downriver again, and then up one of the narrow streets—it, too, was due to be knocked down that autumn. They pushed her gently toward a gate with wire netting nailed above and below it. Then they could only wait and hope. Kathleen glanced over the gate, stopped and looked again.

Patchie's puppies were by then about three months old. She was sitting in the middle of the yard, looking charming but harassed, while puppies seethed and fought and rolled

in every other inch of it. It was clear that Yeff or one of his
fellows had managed to jump the gate after all. Almost
every puppy had a cream-white coat and red ears.

Kathleen put her shopping basket carefully on the pavement. Then she hooked her fingers in the netting, pressed
her face to it and stared. Sol slipped into the house and
gave Patchie's mistress a nudge. Patchie's mistress remembered that her tea towels would be about dry and she went
out to collect them. Kathleen watched the puppies rush up
to her in a mob bawling to be fed.

"Little hypocrites, I only just fed you!" Patchie's mistress
said. She smiled at Kathleen. "I've got a rare old job on
here, I can tell you."

"I know you have," said Kathleen. "Please—when they're
ready—could I buy one of the puppies?"

"Buy one!" Patchie's mistress exclaimed. "I'm giving
them away! I'd never find homes if I didn't. Look at the
number of them, will you! We nearly went mad when she
had them. Patchie was too young anyway, and she couldn't
feed more than a few, so there was me and Ken and Ken's
Dad and my Mum and Ken's Dad's Mum, all on shift work
feeding bottles to puppies. And I'd thought it was bad
enough when our Ken fished Patchie out of the river! Mind
you, we had a good laugh over it. They're quite old enough
to go now. Come on in and take your pick."

She unlatched the gate and Kathleen stepped gingerly in
among the tumbling puppies. All were appealing. Several
were the image of Patchie. Kathleen sorted carefully
through them. None of them had green eyes of course, but

there was one which had the same yellow eyes as Robin's dog, Fossil. Kathleen picked it up.

"This one. Can't I really pay?"

"No you can't, love. You take her. You've got the best of the lot there, to my mind. Some people say they don't like her eyes, but I tell them they don't know a thing about it. She's as clever as a monkey, that one."

"Thank you, then," said Kathleen. "I'll come and show you how she gets on."

She walked home to Miss Smith's with her basket bumping and dangling off one elbow and the puppy snuggled up in both arms, very much as she had carried the much tinier Sirius.

"My dear, how lovely!" said Miss Smith. "I'd been thinking that what you needed was another puppy."

"It's not for me. It's for you," said Kathleen, and she put the puppy carefully in Miss Smith's lap.

Miss Smith's gnarled hands stroked the red ears. "I see why you got him. Apart from the eyes, he's very like Sirius, isn't he?"

"Yes," said Kathleen. "But it's not a he. It's a she, I'm afraid."

"Better and better!" Miss Smith exclaimed, quite delighted. "Then we'll have puppies." She put the little dog carefully down on the floor. The puppy sniffed at the shiny toes of her shoes. "Leone? Viola? Miranda?" said Miss Smith, trying to think of a name. The puppy ran away sideways from her toes and suddenly threw herself back at them in an all-out attack. "I refuse to call you Patch or Snowy, and Beatrice won't do," Miss Smith said above the puppy's rumbles. "Agnes—no." The puppy found her shoelaces and backed away with one in her mouth, whirring like a rattle, with her tail rotating furiously. "Melpomene? Too grand," decided Miss Smith, laughing as the shoelace came out of her shoe and the puppy scuttled away with it, growling defiantly. Kathleen did not laugh. "What is it?" asked Miss Smith.

"I was just thinking—just noticing—" said Kathleen, "that Sirius needed me to look after him whatever shape he was. Only I didn't notice."

"Where there's need enough, a way can often be found," Miss Smith observed.

Polaris often remarks to Sol that Sirius loses his temper much less often these days. But the one sure way to send him into a flaming rage is to suggest that he find a new Companion. Sirius will not hear of it. The small white sphere circling his goes untenanted, because he hopes that what Miss Smith said is true.

Diana Wynne Jones has been a compulsive storyteller for as long as she can remember. "The ability to surprise has become Jones's signature, as have her unflagging inventiveness and almost uncanny ability to create imaginary worlds," said *School Library Journal*. She has written a novel for adults and several other books and plays for children, including *Witch Week* and the award-winning *Charmed Life, A Tale of Time City*, and *The Lives of Christopher Chant*.

Ms. Jones lives in England with her husband, a professor of English at Bristol University. They have three sons.

WITCH WEEK

Strange things are happening at Larwood House! Flocks of birds are swooping into classrooms out of nowhere and kids have been seen riding flying garden implements. Will the real witch in class 6B please stand up? Or can the legendary enchanter Chrestomanci unmask the culprit...before the Inquisitor does?

A TALE OF TIME CITY

Time City—built eons from now on a patch of space outside time—was designed especially to oversee history, but now its very foundations are crumbling from age. Can two boys save their city—with the help of a Twenty Century girl they've kidnapped from wartime England—before it's too late?

CHARMED LIFE

Eric ("Cat") Chant's older sister Gwendolen is so talented that she's already on Advanced Magic. But the powerful enchanter Chrestomanci, from whom she is determined to take magic lessons, is not impressed—and that makes her furious! As Cat nervously awaits a showdown between the two, Gwendolen plans to unleash a magic so potent and so terrible that it will rock their entire world—and not even Chrestomanci will be able to stop her!

Bullseye Books published by Alfred A. Knopf, Inc.

*She had a passion for horses—and for a life
beyond her dead-end hometown*

NOT ON A WHITE HORSE

by Nancy Springer

For horse-crazy Rhiannon DiAngelo (Ree for short), the lure
of an escaped white Arabian horse hiding somewhere in the
nearby woods is irresistible. She's more than happy to spend
her days searching for the beautiful runaway—life at home
has been tough since her father lost his job. Ree's search leads
her to the horse's owner, kindly blacksmith Chickie Miller,
and to another horse who desperately needs her help. With
plenty of encouragement from Chickie, Ree discovers that
she really does have a special feel for horses and slowly nurses
her charge back to health. But best of all, she realizes that her
most cherished dream of working with horses can come
true—*if* she's willing to make it happen.

"The author's honest style makes this a vivid and compelling
novel."   *—Publishers Weekly*

"Intriguing and just introspective enough while still allowing
plenty of action."   *—The Horn Book*

A Bullseye Book published by Alfred A. Knopf, Inc.

They traded identities—and altered their destinies forever!

SEARCHING FOR SHONA

A story of adventure and mystery by award-winning author Margaret J. Anderson

It's the start of World War II, and shy, wealthy Marjorie Malcolm-Smith, along with hordes of other children, is about to be evacuated from Edinburgh. Then, in the midst of the crowded train station she spots a casual acquaintance, a girl named Shona. The two cook up the most brilliant adventure scheme ever—they exchange identities, with the promise to switch back at the end of the war. In the blink of an eye, Shona is off to Canada and Marjorie's rich family, while Marjorie is packed off to the country with Shona's rather meager possessions—including the only clue to Shona's true ancestry. Unexpectedly the war drags on, leaving Marjorie, who's happy in her new life, with the time to unravel the mystery of Shona's past. But the most compelling mystery of all is this: who *is* the real Shona after years have gone by? And what if she doesn't want to switch back?

"Anderson's simple, stark prose is most expressive."
—School Library Journal

"Cleverly conceived." *—Booklist*

A Bullseye Book published by Alfred A. Knopf, Inc.